DARK STARMAGE BOOK 1

Patricia Jones
A.P. Gore

To my lovely Family!
Copyright @ Patricia Jones
ISBN-13:
978-1718771116
ISBN-10:
1718771118

Chapter 1

VISAKA

Roaring thunder crackled inside Visaka's mind. Her longing for home deepened as she scanned the holographic image of a lush green planet, but she knew it was futile. Titan, her home, was lost to her. Forever.

She zoomed in on the image. The large academy building, which could also be seen through space, called her back. She had spent a good amount of her youth inside that building, learning magic. Ten years wasn't a long time in a mage's life, but that decade was the most special one in hers. She wanted to go back there, to re-run those vast corridors that opened the doors to hundreds of classrooms, to recollect her memories at least once before she died in one of her many space battles.

"How many days will you continue to look for your lost memories?" Melinda stood behind her. She must have walked into Visaka's cube while she was busy observing the lush planet.

"I never tire of looking at it, but trust me, this time I accidentally triggered it." Visaka tapped a button, and the holograph disappeared back into the small cube.

"Don't lie, kiddo. I know you miss your home. Even I wish to go back there someday and meet my sisters and brothers."

Melinda sighed. "I guess that's not possible anymore." Sorrow was palpable in her voice.

"Why can't we go back, Melinda? You know I didn't kill him! I don't even remember firing that spell. Everything that happened in that moment feels disjointed and painful." Her body tensed as she remembered her anger... shooting the level two magic spell... Prince Victor falling...

Melinda touched her shoulder. "Relax. I trust you, kiddo. That's why I'm here, on your side, but the recording shows something different, doesn't it? It shows you killing the Crown Prince of Spectra 33."

Melinda was right. There was clear proof of Visaka's crime, but how could a level two air bolt manage to kill a mage of his caliber? There had to be something wrong with the footage.

"I don't know how, but one day I will prove my innocence." Or she should just give up on her dream of going back and live her life in exile.

"Captain!" Bradok, her ship's engineer, shouted over the comms.

"What is it?" Visaka asked.

"Incoming. I'm detecting a Royal Navy ship ten light hours away."

Visaka turned to face her sergeant. "Melinda, cloak the ship."

Melinda nodded and hurried out.

Visaka waited for Melinda to disappear from view, then wrapped the holographic cube in a soft cloth, then placed it in her wardrobe to make sure it wouldn't be broken by the impact of the orbiter vibrations they were about to experience.

"ARE WE INVISIBLE?" Visaka asked after she entered the control bridge.

"Yes, but they may have a spellradar. The intruder ship seems to be of orbiter scout class," Bradok said.

"Let's keep our anti-missile turrets ready. We may need to fire them at any time." Visaka tapped a button to bring up the magic-interfacer. Four threads emerged from it and connected to her head, giving her access to all the ship's systems. Now she could see the incoming ship clearly.

What are they doing here?

This place was enchanted with ancient magic that made ships disappear to who knows where. It was a dead zone where no one in their right mind ever came. If their pilot didn't know what they were looking for, their whole ship could be lost, never to be found again. And yet a scout ship was roaming here.

A wave of vibration passed through the outer shell of the ship and into her body. She focused, sensing an invisible laser piercing the ship's defenses.

"We're spotted. Prepare for incoming." The words had no sooner left her mouth than Visaka saw ten missiles inbound. "Bradok, try a few anti-missiles, but be ready with the spellcannon."

Her ship was old, its anti-missile system rudimentary at best. If the inbound missiles were enhanced with magic, their anti-missile system would fail, miserably. The first five anti-missiles fired by Bradok did nothing but scratch the surface of the enemy missiles, confirming Visaka's fears. The missiles were magically enhanced.

"What choice do we have, Sergeant Melinda? Flee, or fight?" Visaka asked as a formality, because she knew what Melinda would answer. They could return fire and destroy the scout ship with some effort, but if it had backup on the way, they'd be in trouble. She'd been running from trouble for the last three years, and she had no interest in getting into more. Flee, it was.

Bradok shot a fireball—a level-two spell—from the ship's spellcannon and destroyed all ten missiles.

"Hyperdrive in ten, nine..." Visaka's voice shattered as an invisible missile hit the ship. "Damn! they fired a cloaked missile too." She'd missed it because her ship didn't have a spell-radar.

She accessed the system's health information, spotting damage to the oxygen module. That was bad for them; they already lacked a converter mage, and now they were leaking oxygen, too.

"Captain, another ship has jumped in nearby, fifteen light hours from us," Bradok said.

"Damn! This is bad." She had sensed it with her interface, too. It was a cruiser class, one they couldn't fight. That would be suicide.

Chapter 2

RAIDEN

The space station had orbited gradually around the third planet for two thousand years. It hadn't heard a footfall inside it for hundreds of years, but that day it was shaken awake by the cries of a woman.

"Raiden, are you alive?" the woman cried.

Raiden thought he heard Anna, but why was she calling from a faraway place? He tried to open his eyes, but they were stuck together as if they'd been glued shut.

After a while, with an inhuman effort and his face bathed in sweat, he managed to open his eyes. The time he took opening his eyes felt like an eternity.

A black metallic mask with only three holes—two for the eyes and one for the nose—was staring at him.

He shook his head to focus, certain he must be dreaming or something. Still, the mask remained there, and it wasn't a demon. He spotted the blue, dreamy eyes of his fiancée, Anna, visible behind the mask for a split second when a light passed by. In the next flash of light, he saw her full lips quivering under the glass surface of the mask that started from below her nose and extended towards her neck. She sat on her knees, her hands behind her back. Judging from her position, Raiden was sure she was tied up.

"Anna..." His tongue couldn't manage anything more. He coughed and spat up blood. Everything started blurring again, and there was a sharp pain in his neck, throbbing and intense, like there was a metal rod piercing his skin.

Where am I?

"It's okay, babe. I spat blood, too. It'll pass. Look at me and focus." She spoke calm words, but the voice behind those words shook and cracked.

Anna's voice eased him a little and helped to focus his attention on her eyes, but the pain was too powerful to ignore completely.

Then all the confidence Anna had mustered fell apart, and she sobbed frantically.

"Don't cry, please!" Now it was his turn to calm her down, but at the same time, he had questions. "Do you know where we are?"

"Oh God, I thought you were dead. Those guys inserted something into your neck. I was so afraid you were going to die. But Holy Mary saved you from the demons, my love."

Now he understood the cause of his pain. He tried to lift his hands, but they were too numb to move.

Her voice calmed down after a moment. "One of them said something about Earth being frozen long ago... I couldn't understand them properly, but they said something about lifting us and un-freezing us from Earth. Does that make any sense to you, babe?"

By that time, his eyes had adjusted to the miniature lighting. He glanced around to find himself in a room. The color on the walls was torn apart, rusted metal showing through from multiple cracks. They seemed to be held hostage in some old warehouse.

Yes, they were being held hostage. Otherwise, why would Anna be tied to something, a mask covering her face? Now he felt the chain around his hands. He tried to move his hand again, but it was akin to shifting a large boulder, unaided. They must have been here for hours, if not days; his muscles were too stiff to move. But who could have done it? Someone from his past?

It had been two years since he'd left his covert operative job with the U.S. Military, and he'd never had an enemy during his term in Afghanistan. Heck, he'd killed everyone he'd aimed at. Also, some terrorist from Afghanistan coming to imprison them was out of the question. Why would they come to the USA just to kill an insignificant marine?

"Babe, we've been captured by two demons, and I've no idea where we are." Anna took a break from crying, and he was glad that she could recover fast. If they were going to get out of there, they needed to be calm and figure out a solution.

"Don't worry, my love. I don't know where we are, but I'll get us out of here. I promise." It was a promise he meant to keep until his last breath.

A voice emanated from one corner of the room; someone was talking. His eyes snapped open and swiveled in that direction, remaining open to absorb the sight of two men—no, two men with tails and faces that resembled demons in the movies—flying into the room.

"What the fuck?" He couldn't believe what he was witnessing. He moved his head frantically left and right, hoping to escape the influence of whatever vile drug he'd been doped with.

"Raiden, I need to tell you something before we die." She took a deep breath. "It's something I can't hide when I know we'll both be dead soon."

"Shut up, human." The larger creature landed next to Anna and grabbed her neck, lifting her in the air.

"Put her down, or I'll tear you apart." Rage surged through Raiden's bones, and with an immense effort he wrenched his hands free from the chains. But as soon as he did that, he floated in the air, as if he was in a low gravity chamber.

The other creature laughed at him and brought him down by his leg. He tied Raiden again with the chains. "I'm going to kill you after I convert her. But before that, I want you to watch her scream."

"I said, get your hands off her." Raiden squeezed his hand out of the chains and pulled his pistol from his boot, firing a 9mm enhanced bullet at the large creature holding Anna. The bullet traveled at the speed of sound, but it was deflected before reaching its target. It smacked into the wall next to him and floated in the air without much sound, which was kind of strange. The walls were metal, and they should have made the familiar ka-ching sound when the bullet hit.

"Egtholar, I'm converting her. Once done, kill that lowlife. He is of no use to us. His body is showing no sign of the dark energy around him, and we have no use for failures."

The other one, the one with a complex name, pierced Raiden's neck with his tail, and Raiden lost all his energy in one go. He floated in the air. The earlier pain was nothing compared to that caused by the creature's tail, and he couldn't even lift a finger. He could only look on and see what was happening to Anna.

"Raiden..." Anna's voice trembled with pain.

Raiden couldn't say a single word. He just lay there, numb. He watched the big creature insert a black rod into Anna's neck. Surprisingly, Anna's body seemed to swallow it inside once the head was inserted into her skin.

Anna screamed, but Raiden couldn't take his eyes off her. Emptiness crawled inside him. He was no good for anyone. He was useless.

The space all around them started heating up, and he felt an unknown energy radiating through his body, especially through his neck, where the strange sensation of metal remained present inside him. A light emerged from Anna's body, and she rose into the air without any support at all. A light dome with a thick black border covered her entirely; she was emitting the light that formed the dome herself, and it remained active for a moment before resorbing into her. She fell sharply after that, unconscious, floating just a few inches above the surface.

Raiden finally found his voice. "Anna!"

"A gem, Egtholar, a real gem. The Master will be happy to see her. Who could have anticipated a black mage would be hidden in this void?" the big creature said. "Now kill the lowly human and get the receptor out. We can't waste one on this specimen." He looked down at Raiden with darkened, red eyes.

"Anna!" Raiden screamed again, managing to move his hand, but the chains only tightened further. "Let me go, you bastards. I'm going to kill you both!"

A ball of fire hit the creature closest to him. The creature stumbled and cried out in pain. The corner of the room lit up again, and four people exploded into the space, throwing energy balls toward Raiden. He closed his eyes to brace for impact yet felt nothing but a slight touch of electricity passing away from his body. He opened his eyes again to find a blue lightning ball heading towards the smaller creature's head. Its red eyes flashed with yellow light just before it batted the energy ball away with its wing-like hands.

"Egtholar, let's go back. We can't fight here, and we need to get this human to our Master." The large creature jumped back, waved his hands to create a grimy, dark portal, and then flew away through it. He took Anna with him, too.

Raiden's eyes jumped toward the space where he had spied Anna just a moment back, and he saw a couple of fiery energy balls passing through the same area where the big creature and Anna had been. Nothing was there now, only empty space, and the energy bolts passed through it all.

Egtholar, the other creature, followed the bigger one and vanished through a similar portal, leaving Raiden behind.

"Visaka, come here. We have a survivor." A soft hand touched Raiden's face, pulling it up to look in his eyes. Two bright red eyes peered at him from behind a mask. He remembered the creature had red eyes too, but these eyes were relaxing, giving him hope.

"Melinda, he could be a dark mage, so be careful," the other woman said.

"No, he can't be. His eyes are still human and..."

That was the last Raiden heard before fading off into an unknown darkness.

Chapter 3

VISAKA

"Cork, use instant transmission, and us get away from here the moment missiles close on us," Visaka said. "Bradok, quickly check the hyperdrive. We will jump into hyperspace after four transmissions hops."

Visaka's heart started pumping more blood through her heart. She was going to let Cork connect to the ship, and with his lightning magic, he would transport the whole ship to a desired location in space in an instant. It was a quite complex process which only she, being a jumper class mage, could do.

Cork nodded and channeled his magic through the nearest control cube.

Visaka felt Cork's magic entering the ship's system, and she diverted all of it to the ship's hull. The ship instantly teleported few hundred miles away from their current location. A few hundred miles of distance was the limitation of Cork's transportation magic.

"One more time, Cork."

Cork poured his magic into the control cube again, and the ship jumped forward. It continued for four more teleports, and the interface threads retreated from Visaka's neck. She was out of magic.

"Bradok, fire the hyperdrive now." There was nothing more she could do. She let herself relax in the pilot's chair as the adrenaline rush faded.

Space around her smoothed out, an indication of being in hyperspace. Now they were traveling at more than light's speed, fast enough to get them out of enemies' reach.

"Oxygen, we need it," Visaka said. "What's the nearest habitable planet which is not governed by the mage emperor?"

"Venus, the first planet in the almost dead solar system. Strangely, our database indicates it is an unreachable destination. I wonder why." Melinda said.

"I know why," Visaka said. "We are heading to the first vessel, then. It will let us access that planet."

When she was ten years old, Visaka had visited this solar system on a special mission with her father. Her father had shown her how to access the first vessel's controls and open the portal to Venus through the protective ward placed by the first mage emperor. The first vessel was a space station built by the mage emperor when he left Venus two thousand years back. No one knew why he did it, but he cast a spell around that entire solar system that hid all nine planets. Her father thought it unnecessary, since no one came to the dead space.

"CAPTAIN, THERE ARE some odd signals coming out of the first vessel." Sergeant Cork stared at the space station roaming around the dead star called Sun.

"Who in the world would have come to visit this damned system?" Visaka whispered. Their oxygen supply was waning rapidly. They had two choices: die without oxygen, or take a chance and fight whoever was on the first vessel. She chose the second option.

"Unless one of you can convert our farts into oxygen, we're in for a fight." Visaka pulled up the sensor data on her screen. "Oh, this is good news. We only have two body signatures." She smiled until her eyes darted to the energy-type analysis. "God, this can't be true…"

"What is it, kid?" Melinda peeked at her screen.

Melinda was her closest friend on the ship, and she had a nagging habit of calling Visaka things like her name, kid, or kiddo rather than Captain. Visaka didn't like it, but what could she do? Melinda knew her from her childhood, and she respected her far too much to complain about such a small thing.

Visaka gave Melinda an unsmiling look. "Two dark mages. Why don't you use your fire magic and check if there are any dark creatures present too?"

Melinda nodded, pulled magic from within herself, and spread it across the first vessel.

Visaka watched as Melinda closed her eyes and started receiving the response from her magic. Melinda's specialty magic was life magic, and she could spread her fire magic even in vacuum and detect the presence of humans or dark creatures around a wide area.

"Only two dark mages, but are you sure it's wise to go in there when the dark mages are there?" Melinda raised her usual worrying doubt.

"You very well know if we don't get to Venus, we can't make it to the outer ring of the neutral world. Why would you ask such a silly question in our hour of need?" Visaka replied in a disappointed tone. There was another reason, too. The moment she heard about dark mages, her blood had started rushing in anticipation of an epic fight. How could she miss the opportunity of lifetime?

Melinda made some silly sound that Visaka decided to ignore.

"The dark mages," Visaka said. "It's been a while since I have heard about them. We can't miss this, Melinda, certainly not."

"I haven't heard of them visiting our side in one hundred years." Melinda looked more serious than she ever was. "There is another strange thing I noticed. There are two humans present on that space station along with the dark mages."

"Can this be their meeting place?" Visaka asked. Were these humans working as spies for the dark mages? It wasn't unheard of. But why would they choose this place as their meeting place? It made little sense.

"Melinda, prepare the small transport. We are going in. Also, Bradok, we will need as much as firepower as we can get."

"Captain, we can't leave this ship empty," Cork said. "What if someone spots us? We should leave Bradok on the ship."

"No, we can't leave him behind when we are facing dark mages. We need his fire magic to fight them." Visaka worried what kind of power these dark mages would have.

"I just hope this works," Melinda whispered and walked away to prepare the shuttle for launch.

"ON MY MARK," VISAKA murmured.

As the shuttle moved closer to the docking station of the first vessel, Visaka donned her air mask and applied air magic to her shoes. It was a level one spell which allowed her maneuver through zero gravity places. She repeated it for Melinda, Bradok, and Cork. The moment the shuttle docked in the still-functioning airlock, they all jumped aboard and ran toward the room where they had detected the dark mages.

The first vessel was made up of some old metal, and with a couple thousand years of wear and tear, it was falling apart, but Visaka could feel the majesty's magic holding it together even after so many years.

She slowed when they got closer to their destination and walked the rest of the way. Sneaking into the room, she found a small dark mage conjuring a darkness spell in his hands. An injured human male lay in front of him. The spell the dark mage was casting had a thick outer shell around its core magic—a level three spell, if she wasn't mistaken. If he hit the human with that spell, he would be shredded to pieces.

She waved at Bradok, who quickly conjured a level two fireball and shot it toward the mage. Visaka gave the fireball a little push with air magic to accelerate it. The fireball traveled through the air in blink of an eye and hit the dark mage square on his head, making him lose concentration, but her air bolt had no effect on the dark mage beyond stopping his spell conjuration.

She pulled her magic into her hands and fired another spell, a level four air ball. It had the potential to really hurt the creature, but he nullified her spell with an equally strong purple energy bolt.

The other dark mage, who was holding the human female, was under the barrage of fireballs and lightning spears from her crew, but none of their spells fazed him. He seemed to be stronger than they'd anticipated. He said something to his companion, then opened a portal to the fourth dimension. For the moment the portal was open, Visaka felt the dark energy tendrils jumping out of the portal, shooting for the closest human mage: Melinda. The portal edges illuminated when the creature disappeared inside it, then shrunk down to a tiny hole before vanishing completely.

Visaka's breath eased as the dark portal closed down. The fourth dimension wasn't a pleasant place for a human mage. "Melinda, be wary, these mages are using the fourth dimension!" Visaka rushed forward before the other dark mage could vanish with the remaining human. She needed to know what they were doing there. If they were colluding, she could inform the authorities.

Cork jumped forward, a level four ball of lightning swirling in his hand. This was a specialty of Cork's; he could continuously channel his magic and maintain the lightning ball's swirling until he got to point-blank range of the target. Ball lightning had immense magic in it, but it lacked speed and was used more as a close combat spell.

The remaining dark mage retreated and then vanished into the fourth dimension.

Visaka stared at the place of the dark portal longer than required. The dark mages had vanished without giving her any information on why they were here. If only she could call King Gordon directly. She thought for a moment, then shook her head. That boat had sailed a long time ago. There'd be no going back to the King of Spectra 33.

Melinda checked on the human lying on the ground. She pulled his face up and looked in his eyes.

"Visaka, this one is alive, and looks to be human still. What should we do about him?"

"Let's take him back to the ship," Visaka said.

"But Captain," Cork said. "He could be a dark mage! He still has the receptor inside his body, and by the looks of the place, they were running an initiation ritual here."

"We will deal with him if he turns out to be a dark mage," Visaka replied, turning back to retreat to her ship. Bradok channeled his magic to open a portal to Venus as she'd instructed before leaving their ship. Venus was the only planet in this solar system which had the oxygen supply they needed to survive, the only living planet left in this dead solar system.

Chapter 4

VISAKA

"Bradok, how much time it will take to open the portal?" Visaka asked as soon as they docked their shuttle in the *Challenger*, the ship she owned.

"Five hours. The system is old and can't take more magic."

"Not optimal, but okay. We have other preparations to make before we land on Venus. I wonder what surprises might be waiting for us this time. Last time I visited Venus with my father, we encountered a large lizard which was tough to kill." For more than one thousand years, nature had run wild on the planet, making it green and lush, even more so than Titan, her home planet.

"Captain, what about the human we bought with us? I don't think it was a wise decision. He could be a spotty dipshit dark mage in the making," Cork muttered in his own crazy tone.

"Language, Brother," Bradok warned.

"And what should I have done? Left him to die there?" Visaka raised her brows. She didn't like being questioned. She could have cut Cork's tongue out for challenging her, if only she was in her palace on Titan.

"Maybe..." Cork said.

"What if I had done the same with you in the battle of Amara?" Visaka asked. "Don't give me bullshit!"

"Cork, why don't you go and make the count of things we can fulfill from Venus?" Bradok said.

Cork nodded and left.

Melinda placed her hand on Visaka's shoulders to calm her down. "He is naive and untrained."

"True, but I should have my anger under control. I'm not a princess anymore." Her thoughts wandered to the past, but Bradok's next sentence pulled her back to the present.

"You will always remain a princess to us, Ma'am," Bradok chipped in.

Visaka stared at him. He was wiser of the brothers. He was a phalanx class man who believed in loyalty more than anything else, and he had proved it to her multiple times.

"Thanks, Bradok," Visaka said. Their loyalty meant a lot to her.

"But the question remains, why did you bring him here?" Melinda asked.

"I just couldn't let him die there. Even if he turns out to be a dark mage, better to kill him by my own hands than leave him on an abandoned space station to suffocate."

"I don't understand," Melinda said. "What was he doing there? And who was the other woman with those two mages? I'm dead sure that there were two humans. My magic doesn't lie to me." She paused. "Maybe they were under initiation when my magic was spread around the space station and hence evaded Cork's spell."

Melinda had a point. If the Dark mages were performing the initiation process, that would have made these humans go undetected by her magic. "But if that was the case, they wouldn't have left this human behind. They are very particular about not leaving their mages in the open like this. I bet this man is a spy."

"If he were a spy, he wouldn't have been chained to the wall. And the first dark mage was conjuring a darkness spell to kill him," Melinda said.

"Let's check his aura lines. I think he didn't pass through conversion."

"Good point. I will get my magic meter and meet you in the medical bay," Melinda added and walked out.

WHEN VISAKA ENTERED the medical bay, Melinda was already attaching the threads of the magic meter to the man's head and chest. She always wondered why Melinda carried a magic meter on the ship when they had no use for it. It was mainly used at the academy to measure the magical potential of new students.

Melinda adjusted some settings on her device and poured some fire magic into it. The device shook with energy, and the same energy flew into the human's body. The device was simple. It used the caster's magic to measure the resistance the target put against it. By using that resistance, the magic potential of the target was calculated.

"This is odd," Melinda said after struggling with the device for a few minutes.

"What is odd? Is he turning into a dark mage?" Visaka conjured an air spell on her palm.

"No. There is no trace of any dark magic in his body."

"What is the issue, then?"

"He doesn't have any magic at all. My magic energy flew like a free rain through his body, but then there are two aura lines around his heart going out in different directions. It's like he has opposite waves of magic originating from his heart." Melinda rolled her eyes. "I have never seen such a thing before."

"This isn't possible. He must have at least few thousand aura lines. Maybe this device is broken," Visaka replied. Her mind delved into the theory of aura lines she had studied many years back. Even a mage with a very low level of magic would have thousands of aura lines emerging from her heart. This wasn't possible. In theory.

"Bradok, do we have any spell'O'armor lying around?" Visaka turned to face him.

"Yes, an old type. But for whom? We don't have any marines around," Bradok asked.

"We should test the armor on this man once we land on Venus. If the magic meter is broken, we can test it using the spell'O'armor," she said, thinking about the man lying on the berth who had started moving his finger as they talked. "Melinda, be prepared. He is waking up."

Melinda was already readying her magic in her right hand. She was at point-blank range. Even a dark mage wouldn't be able to withstand her magic at that distance.

With lots of difficulty, the man opened his eyes and looked at Visaka. He looked to be in his mid-thirties, but a subtle beard made him look older. He had ocean blue eyes, a sharp nose, well-built muscles, and eyes that could penetrate the heart easily.

"Who are you?" Visaka asked, studying the man who was having difficulty moving his body around.

He stared at her in surprise, and a moment later he turned his eyes away. "I'm Raiden. Are you the one who stormed into that old building? Do you have Anna as well?" Hope lurked within his eyes.

"Who is Anna?" Visaka asked. "The girl taken by the dark mage?" There was something odd about everything here, but she couldn't point out exactly what it was.

"My fiancée, the woman with me. We were planning to get married soon, but then I woke up in that building, and—" His eyes jumped to Melinda and locked on her spell. "What is that? How can she do that?" He stared at the fireball swirling in Melinda's hand with his mouth wide open.

"That's magic. What's surprising about that?" Melinda asked.

"When did humans learn magic? Am I dreaming or something?" He rubbed his eyes.

Visaka grabbed his shirt and pulled him to her eye level. "Human, who are you? Where are you from?"

"I told you. I'm Raiden. I live in California." He met her eyes, unblinking.

For a man in the medical bay of an unknown ship, at the mercy of an unknown person, he surely had guts.

"And which Spectra is this California from?" Visaka asked. "Are you a spy? Give me the truth, and I may spare your life."

"What... Spectra? California, USA... The biggest country in the whole world?"

His expression confused her more. She searched her memories, trying to find anything that resembled that name, but whatever planet this USA was, it was out of her reach.

Melinda tapped at a nearby display device. "Wait a moment, do you mean United States of America? A country from the old planet, Earth?"

"Yes, but why old Earth? Are you from outer space? That does make sense, magic... even those demons said something about lifting us from Earth—" He paused and looked between them. "But neither of you look like aliens." Raiden's eyes expanded with curiosity again.

"No, it's not possible," Visaka said. Planet Earth was no longer a living planet for humanity. On Venus, her father had told her the story of their ancestors who'd lived on Earth. Two million years ago, some unknown magic had frozen the planet and the humans on it. People who had settled on Venus were the only survivors. Many attempts were made to revive those humans on Earth, but none succeeded. That's why the first mage emperor declared the solar system a dead zone and left it to find more suitable planets. Yet this man claimed he was from Earth. How was that even possible?

Chapter 5

ANNA

"Who are you? Where am I?" Anna stood in front of a man wearing a black suit, or was it armor?

"Kneel, slave." The creature that had brought her kicked her shin, and she fell on her knees. He chuckled. "That's better."

"Master, what is your next order?" another creature asked.

"What do they call you on that lowly planet of yours?" The one called Master spoke with a voice deeper than the sea and more frightening than a ghost.

"Anna. My name is Anna."

"Magita, that's your new name going forward."

"Who are you? And what are these things?" She looked at the two creatures standing nearby, their tail moved as if it had its own will.

The master laughed. "You are my pawn, Magita, and I expect you to obey me. Now show me your powers. Egtholar, trigger her."

The small creature grabbed her throat. His other hand glowed with purple energy. She tried to avoid the energy ball coming towards her stomach. Her body vibrated as the energy ball closed in on her.

There she was, about to get killed by an energy ball. She missed Raiden. If he had been there, she would have lived to tell the tale.

She grasped for breath as a sharp burning pain consumed her. The pain grew to the point that she couldn't bear it anymore. She waited for sweet death to wrap her in its comfy hands, but even death didn't come to rescue her. Her own power came. A strange energy radiated from her heart and spread across her body. The earth below her liquefied, and the next moment she and the creature holding her dissolved into the ground.

The creature's eyes widened. "Don't leave my hand!"

Anna didn't know what was happening. She looked up and wished to be above the ground. Her wish was granted by some unknown God. The next moment, she stood on the surface, but the creature that had hurt her was gone. Well, she could see his tail above ground, so he was buried alive.

She stepped back in fear. "Did I do that?"

"Dead, inside the earth. Good, we got an earth mage." The master stared at her. "Telenoth, I entrust her training to you. The next time I see her, I want to see a powerful mage." He vanished through a black portal, the same portal they had traveled through.

"What is this power swirling inside me?" she asked Telenoth. It was a lot to take, but she liked the way it made her feel. "What did you do with Raiden?" She remembered Raiden as a distant memory. Something had changed inside her, and she was losing his memory to a black fog. Was it something these creatures did to her?

Chapter 6

RAIDEN

Raiden opened his eyes to find a short man with broad shoulders poking his arm with a weird-looking axe. The axe had two heads, pointing in opposite directions. He remembered seeing something like that in a fantasy movie, once upon a time.

When the man noticed Raiden was awake, he swung his axe and tapped Raiden's forehead with the metal knob.

"So, you are the puny Earthling who doesn't have any magic, huh? I never thought I would see an Earthling in my whole life." Curiosity lurked in his eyes, but there was hatred too, hatred which sent cold waves through Raiden's veins. "Heck, I didn't even know this Earth even existed."

Raiden had witnessed similar killer instincts in Afghanistan, and that didn't sit well with him. "Who're you?"

He looked around for something to defend himself with if this man decided to kill him. There was nothing in sight that he could use as a weapon, only a small stool, a small commode, and a sink with couple of tabs. Seeing the water made him realize he was hungry and thirsty at the same time.

When was the last time I ate something?

"I'm Cork, Sergeant of the ship. I came here to make one thing clear, dark mage. I don't trust you. I'm just waiting for a chance to kill you. Is that clear?"

"I'm not a dark mage. I'm just a normal human who lost his fiancée to the weird creatures you call dark mages."

"Oh, yes, your woman," Cork replied. "So, what are you going to do about her?"

"I'm going to get her back, of course. How do I do that?" Raiden asked, but he wasn't sure if this man would help him.

"Forget her."

"Why?" Raiden's face hardened. "She's my life, and you want me to forget her?" He missed Anna, and every moment he was awake he spent puzzling over how to find her and get her back. He'd had a long discussion with the captain of the ship, and apparently the Earth was frozen a thousand years back. He and Anna weren't supposed to be alive. But it wasn't his fault if he was revived by those bastard mages who took his Anna away from him. "Just tell me how to get her back."

"You can't. No one will help you with that either. Dark mages live far away. Even with a hyperdrive, you can't get there. Who in the world knows what they have done with your woman? If I were you, I would have forgotten about her long ago and cared about what's next for me," Cork said with a grimy tone.

"What's next for me?" Raiden raised his eyes to meet Cork's. Cork was probably a terrifying man, but he had faced many bullies like him in the military and taught them a lesson they deserved. He would make sure that Cork got his lesson too, someday.

"If it was up to me, I would have already thrown you out on some asteroid. We don't have space and food for a bastard fucker like you."

"There must be something you can help me with." Cork was getting on his nerves, but he had to remain calm and think a way out of this. There had to be something he could do to save Anna. If magic existed, that meant there would be a magical item or a mage who could help him to get Anna back. He might just have to try harder. His fingers clenched around the chains that bound him, trying to pull them apart.

Cork's weapon moved, and in the blink of an eye its sharp edge was at his throat.

"Cork, stop it already!" A lady with calm red eyes shouted from the opposite side of the room. He remembered her. She was the one who'd saved him back on that space station. She wore an ankle-length white robe and appeared to be in her mid-forties, although she seemed to have lot more experience than that.

"Melinda, what are you doing here?" Cork stared at the lady, then pulled his axe away from Raiden's throat.

Raiden looked at Melinda with gratitude.

"Saving your ass from Captain's peril. Did you forget what she said about touching the prisoner?" Melinda asked.

Raiden was a prisoner, even though the captain was nice to him when they'd talked for almost an hour.

"Can I have some water? Beer, if you have any?" Raiden asked as Melinda walked closer.

"What is beer?" Melinda asked. "We don't have anything called that on this ship. I have food and water for you. If you promise not to try anything stupid, I may just remove the chains from your hand." Her voice was calm.

"I promise, I won't do anything stupid. I'm helpless against your magic anyway," Raiden said, still unsure about all the magic stuff.

She started removing his chains, but then she paused and looked in his eyes. "Don't even think about doing something stupid. I don't want to kill you for some stupid reason." Melinda's voice had an edge of deadly warning.

Raiden nodded back. He wouldn't have taken her lightly, anyway.

Melinda handed him a plate with some brown gee stuff in it which looked like mud. He couldn't guess what it was, but when he tasted it, he liked it. It tasted like strawberry cream.

"I'm sorry, but we don't have any oxygen left for making the tasty stuff. Once we land on Venus, we will fill our oxygen cylinders and start producing tasty food which everyone can enjoy."

"Venus and oxygen? Since when does it produce oxygen? I thought Earth was the only planet with an atmosphere in our solar system." He paused. "I don't get it. The last I knew, the humans settled in Venetian colonies had to use artificial converters to produce oxygen." He remembered seeing a documentary on the mission to Venus after sun started dimming exponentially and living on Venus became possible.

"A couple thousand years can do wonders. The planet still wasn't big enough to support the whole of humanity. The mage emperor had to leave that planet for good," Melinda said.

"I could defiantly use a starter course on the last two thousand years of history, and on your magic too." Raiden's mind tried to fill the gaps of what could have happened, but it was too much for him to process, or even imagine.

"WHAT'S THIS?" RAIDEN raised his eyebrows when Melinda threw a small black cube at him.

"That's the spell'O'armor. Not the latest one, but you can manage with it," she replied.

"How does it work?" He couldn't fathom how the cube was armor.

"Just place your hand on it, and it will come to life."

He followed her instruction, and the cube floated in the air, then shot like a bullet toward his heart. He tried to jump back, but before he could even lift his leg, the cube collided with him. He expected pain but felt only the smooth feel of silky black cloth covering his whole body, inch by inch. The cloth stopped just above his neck. When he tried to pinch it, it stiffened under his fingers.

"It will become stiff in response to kinetic energy. Normal bullets and weapons won't work on this."

"It's nice." He touched it again. "But what's special about it?"

"We will test your magic power with the help of this armor. You can fire higher level spell with this armor."

"Levels of magic?" he asked.

"Yes, people start with level one spells, and as their power level increases, they can use higher level spells."

"Wow, that's nice, but I don't have any magic in me. And even if I did, I don't know where to look for it." Was it possible that he had magic from birth, and didn't know about it before now? It sounded like an idiot's idea.

"I will confirm that. Once we land on Venus, we will test your magic," Melinda said with a smile on her face.

Raiden looked at the black armor. It felt nice and comfy from inside, but from outside it looked too grainy to be new. It might have been used by others already. Technology, or magic behind the spell'O'armor was cool, but he didn't understand how it was going to invoke his latent magic power.

"GET YOUR ASS OUT OF the ship. We have landed already." Cork poked Raiden with his axe.

Raiden stood up and followed Cork down corridor after corridor. He was curious about the outside world. If Melinda was right, and Venus had turned into an Earth-like planet, he was in for a treat. If only Anna were here, he could have enjoyed it a lot more. He sighed.

"The armor looks nice on you." Melinda joined them after few corridors and gave him a nice and comforting smile.

He smiled back. The armor fit his body as if it was made for him, but even after wearing it for last few hours he didn't feel any magic evoking inside his body. He shoved the hopeless thoughts aside and followed Melinda out of the airlock, which opened into a dense forest.

The ship maintained day-night cycle, but seeing the actual sunlight made his heart race. "Wow, this is amazing. I can't believe we're on Venus. It feels like..." Raiden wanted to say like home, but it wasn't his home. The forest was green, and the trees were almost forty feet high, but there was unnatural silence present in the forest. His eyes kept darting between the trees to search for wildlife, but there was none. Not even a single bird chirped. The trees had blue fruits, which looked poisonous, and the sun was dimmer than he remembered.

"Raiden, you're here already?"

Visaka, the captain, jumped out of the airlock. She wore a similar suit as him, but it looked new and damn sexy on her in the way it clung to her womanly curves.

"Yes, ma'am." His military training kicked in. Every captain should be given her due respect.

"The armor you are wearing is a spell'O'armor Type Three. It doesn't hold any magic, but it will channel your own magic. It's very useful for low magic marines, who can't really channel their own magic without help. But this won't pull out magic on its own; you have to start it yourself."

"What do you mean by start it, ma'am? How do I do that?"

"Close your eyes. Imagine you are calling upon your magic, and then direct it toward your hands," Melinda said. "It's simple, kid, even a ten-year-old boy can do that easily."

It was frustrating for Raiden to tell them how he felt when they kept telling him that magic was all around and within everyone. "If only I'd had a chance to live in a society full of magical people. Anyway, I'll try." He closed his eyes and tried calling upon his magic. He opened his eyes in hope of finding some form of energy floating around his hands, but there was nothing, not even a spark. "I told you, I don't have any magic."

"Let me give you a boost." The captain walked forward and touched his shoulder.

The moment she touched him, wind flung his body forward. If not for his military training, he would have hurt his face badly by crashing into the tree. A moment before he crashed into the trunk, he extended his legs and bounced back from the tree.

"What was that for? Are you trying to kill me?" he roared and looked at the captain, who smiled.

"I thought I would give it a try, but I think it's of no use." Visaka walked back to the ship with a mischievous smile.

"Is she mad? Why would she do that?" Raiden asked Melinda. He couldn't understand why the captain had thrown him like that, and how could she do it with just a touch.

"She was trying to invoke your magic by brute force. She hoped that your body would invoke the latent magic when you were put in a life-threatening situation. Anyway, that was a failed attempt, so we will try with the Type Three armor next." Melinda walked back to the ship.

Now what should I do here alone?

Raiden decided to explore the jungle. He was curious why there were no birds around. He walked through the trees for around fifty meters, and then he found where were all the birds had gone. A giant bird with almost five-foot-long wings sat on the top of a tree, chewing on another small bird of his kind. It seemed to be that bird's territory.

Raiden slowly backtracked, as he didn't want to be the bird's next meal.

After a while, Melinda came back with another small cube. It looked similar to the one he'd previously worn, though this one had a small display with flashing green bars on it attached to its arm.

"Hey, there's a large bird sitting some hundred meters from here. Shouldn't we go inside?" Raiden asked.

"That? don't worry. We have a proximity shield outside of the ship which repels the local animals. They won't even see us."

"Okay, that's assuring." Raiden's muscles loosened up. "So how does this Type Three armor work?"

"This armor stores magic from a mage, but it still needs the wearer to have some level of magic to direct the suit. I've charged this suit with my magic, and now using your magic you can cast spells." She pointed out a display built on the cube with three green bars. "This is the energy meter." She tapped on his chest at a certain point, and the armor he was wearing retreated into the cube. "Go ahead and try the new one."

He pressed the cube to his chest, and the suit expanded and covered him up to his neck.

"How do I cast the spells again?" he asked.

"Just tap on these buttons. There are even armors which work on thoughts and a built-in HUD, but we don't have any of that on our ship. Now point your hand toward the tree and tap on the button on your chest."

He followed her instructions and tapped on the first button on his chest, but something went wrong. He remembered getting thrown into the air before he lost his consciousness.

Chapter 7

VISAKA

Visaka observed the oxygen meter of her ship slowly filling. Bradok had done an excellent job and fixed the damage to the oxygen module, so it was now working as intended. She hoped to finish refilling the oxygen tanks quickly and travel back to space. If a threat arose on this planet, she didn't have enough manpower to repel it. If she'd had a moleconversion class air mage, she wouldn't have stopped on Venus at all. She was an air mage too, but she had affinity towards flight power. A moleconversion power mage could easily convert one element into another, but those were very rare. One in a thousand people were born with the jumper class, but one in a thousand jumper class mages were born with the transmutation powers, and recruiting one was too much expensive for someone like her.

A red dot on the other screen grabbed her attention. It indicated a couple of animals roaming near the proximity shield she had placed around the ship. The last time she was here, her father had fought a couple of large reptiles. Those animals were deadly and proved to be a tough fight for her father's guards, so she didn't want to take any risk while they filled up the oxygen.

She ignored the red dots and pulled up the footage from the ship's exterior cameras on her screen. She was curious about the training Melinda was giving Raiden with Type Three spell'O'armor. She wanted to see if Raiden really possessed no power, even after being initiated by the dark mages. The fact that Raiden was initiated by a dark mage made her worry a lot, but when she looked in his eyes she found nothing but truth. Still, she had some reservations about trusting that man.

Raiden was trying a spell.

Visaka zoomed in on the energy levels the suit possessed, and the three dots made her worried. That might be too much for him, might hurt him in process.

"What was she was thinking when charging that suit to level three energy?" Visaka jumped out of her chair to run outside. The novice human could kill anyone if he missed the shot he was trying. The three dots, if used properly, could kill ten humans easily. Melinda was naive when she charged the armor that much. *Really, Melinda?*

When she was on the last stretch of the corridor toward the air lock, she heard an explosion.

"God, please don't let anyone die today," she prayed while channeling her magic to increase her speed exponentially.

The first thing she noticed was Cork lying down, maybe dead, his axe flung ten feet away by the impact. Melinda was pushed back against a tree, appearing completely drained from having to create a defensive shield across her to absorb the impact. And the new human, Raiden, was literally hanging on a tree branch.

"What the hell? What just happened?" Her jaw clenched shut as she pulled up the outside camera recordings on a nearby display.

Raiden had misfired the spell. Actually, he couldn't even fire it. The moment he tapped the button on his chest, the power burst out of his suit, sending him flying toward a tree. Cork was caught in the direct impact, and Melinda suffered from a secondary impact generated, but she saved herself by conjuring a defense shield.

"I knew this was a bad idea in the first place." Visaka glanced at Raiden and felt that she should let him die there. He was the reason for this mess, and she didn't like it. She quickly checked on Cork, who was still breathing.

Thank God.

The display near her turned red again. The three animals she had spotted a few minutes back were approaching the ship. She didn't have to worry about them as long as the proximity shield was up. She was about to move and pull Cork to his feet when she noticed the two dots were reaching her position faster.

Visaka rapidly tapped through menus to enter the ship's health dashboard. Their proximity shield had been damaged by the explosion.

"Fuck, not now." She cursed her fate. Now she had to quickly get everyone inside and seal the door. She was almost on top of Melinda, who was the farthest from the ship, when she heard the bloodcurdling sound of a flying creature. Her eyes darted to the sky. A large flying bird with ten feet wings was closing in on her with its mouth wide open. Its sharp teeth sent a chill across her body.

The creature was too close to shoot, so Visaka pulled her magic out and created an air shield around herself and Melinda. Her eyes reacted to another sound, and she found a large leopard-like creature closing on Cork. And then she saw another flying bird was darting toward Raiden.

"God, give me the strength." She pulled her magic in her palms. She had only a few moments before the second creature ate Cork. She instinctively ignored Raiden. Her crew was more important right now.

Visaka waved her hand, and a level two air bolt emerged out of her palm, shooting toward the second creature. Per her calculations, her spell should knock down the creature for good, and she could focus on the third one. But something was amiss. A fourth creature jumped in the path of her air bolt and was knocked down instead, leaving Cork in imminent danger.

Visaka longed for more power, but she was half-drained by the constant use of the air shield. And unless she left Melinda defenseless on the ground, she couldn't run and protect Cork. She had to choose between Melinda and Cork, and she chose Melinda.

The second creature raised his sharp claws to pierce into Cork's body. She wanted to close her eyes and not see what would happen to Cork. But she hadn't needed to, as Raiden jumped on the body of the creature, punched it, and mounted its neck.

The creature jumped back, trying to get Raiden off its back, and it succeeded after a couple of tries. Raiden jumped and landed next to Cork's axe. He easily lifted it in his left hand and bolted toward the creature to slice the axe through its eyes. Visaka noticed his right hand was limp, as if it were broken.

He isn't a waste after all. He is clearly thinking smart.

Visaka turned her focus to the flying bird that kept coming back to beat itself against her shield. This time, Visaka hit it with a level three air scythe, a skill she had perfected in her academic training. She was an air mage, and she could convert the air around her into any shape she dreamed of. Blood burst out of the creature's right wing, and it flew away.

Visaka turned her gaze on Raiden. He was already chopping the head off of the second dead creature.

MELINDA WALKED INTO Visaka's cube. "I'm sorry for the mess, Captain."

Visaka's eyes lingered on Melinda's face. It was a rare situation when Melinda called her by designation, but that meant Melinda understood her error.

"You'd better be," Visaka said with a stern look.

"I know. I should have kept the charge limited to one dot."

"It was like giving a child control of a loaded laser. I'm just thankful that no one got killed. There were at least a dozen possible ways that someone could have ended up dead because of that blast or the carnivorous animals on this planet." Visaka's face flashed with heat as she remembered the sharp teeth of the creature trying to eat Cork.

"I'm sorry again." Melinda looked down. "But that brat is good at weapon handling, isn't he?"

"That was surprising for me as well, especially the way he jumped down from the top of the tree. Anyway, what happened back there confirms that he has no magical power," Visaka added.

"Well, he does have some magical power, but it's just not enough to use any kind of spell'O'armor."

"You'd better not give him that armor again. We may have use for it once we recruit more people," Visaka said, but deep down in her heart she knew it would be rare to find anyone willing to work on her ship.

"Agreed, Captain. " She turned back to walk out of Visaka's cube but stopped mid-way. "One more thing. We will have to spend one more day on the planet to let Bradok fill the ship's magic reserves. He used lot of his magic to get the proximity shield up again."

"Fine by me," Visaka replied.

Chapter 8

RAIDEN

Raiden woke to the sound of someone entering his cube. Yes, he was given a separate cube to sleep after the show he put on with the animals. He was surprised when Visaka allotted him a cube and removed his chains, but maybe he had gained her trust after saving her sergeant on the planet.

"Hey brain-boiled gaylord raper, I came here to say thank you. But don't let that go to your head too much. Because I don't like you, and I won't, not anytime soon." Cork sat on the small stool in the corner. "How is your hand doing, pighead?"

Raiden had broken his hand in the blast, which was quickly fixed by the medical bot of the ship. "I get that, Cork. But it's good to see you smiling occasionally," Raiden replied with a smirk.

"You bastard." Cork laughed, hard. "I watched the complete footage. And I must say buddy, that was a hell of a move you pulled out there. That jump was damn good. No one would believe that you pulled that off without battle armor or magic. Only air mages can do that sort of thing."

"Well..." Raiden thought about it for a moment. "I was trained in physical combat back on Earth." Raiden was a military veteran, but that wasn't always a good thing back on Earth, and Cork didn't need to know that, either.

"Were you a marine or something?" Cork asked.

"No. But how do you know about marine training? You guys know magic and can shoot fireballs from your hands. Why would you need marines or soldiers?" Raiden asked.

"It's true that we know magic, but only one in ten people have enough battle usable magic. So, we have marines, who have magic, but not like us mages. Marines are trained in physical combat, like you, and a few are trained in magical combat with spell'O'armor Type Three."

"So, there is no one in this world without magic in them?" Raiden asked, feeling a bit out of place.

"You can say something like that." Cork's face turned hard, "I know man, it's going to be hard for you, to live in a world full of magic. So, you'd better prepare yourself."

Raiden's face hardened. He knew he was the odd man out amongst these people, but he had just learned that he was the odd man out in the entire world.

How am I going to find you, my love?

Chapter 9

MELINDA

Melinda walked into Raiden's cube and found him playing with the display in there. "Come on, brat, let's try some magic."

"With you?" Raiden jumped from the stool and almost dropped the display in his hand when he heard her.

"Yes, with me. Meet me outside. We're going to conjure some magic." She hated repeating things.

"But, I don't have magic in me. We proved that already." His eyes were sad and downcast.

Melinda thought for a moment. "I don't know, brat, but I believe you've got some magic." She felt for him, because she knew the pain of having no magic. Her own brother was one of the rarest people living in this universe who contained very little magic, and that had put him through a lot of difficult turns already. When she noticed this kid also couldn't do any magic, her heart was pulled to him automatically.

"Are you sure about it? Is it safe here?" Raiden looked around.

"Are you crazy, kid? The Captain would kill me if we tried anything here. We will do this outside when everyone is busy with something or another. I have found a little blind spot for the ship, and there are no animals around to worry about, either. We will walk out of the proximity field to avoid any damage. Not that you could repeat the fiasco again, as we will be trying only a simple elemental spell," She smiled.

Raiden seemed relaxed after hearing that.

They took the east way out of the ship. Melinda tapped her code in the airlock and they exited into a valley.

"I thought we landed in a forest," Raiden said.

"Not actually. We landed in a small fissure on the planet's surface. Upper deck opens in the forest, and the storage dock opens in the valley."

"Wow. How big is this ship?" Raiden turned back to face the ship, but he couldn't comprehend the size of it with his bare eyes.

"Hmm, I don't have all the details. We just recently bou—" She bit her lip. Raiden didn't need to know where they'd bought the ship. "Anyway, let's focus on conjuring a level one spell. If we were starting from basic training you would've undergone physical and mental capability tests and adjusted your course accordingly, but here we will just do it."

"Okay, but first tell me how to perform a spell? You people keep saying to call it from inside, but from where? Do I have some pocket inside my mind where I can find the magic? Or inside my body somewhere? Come on, you have to give me something." Raiden scrubbed his right hand over his face.

"Hmm." She remembered her learning days. Everyone could conjure a basic level one spell when they turned eight, three years after they underwent the initiation. The ones who couldn't learn basic magic on their own learned it in school, and there they had all sorts of equipment to help the kids get their magic flowing. But even the poorest kid had thousands of magic lines emerging from their heart, and this kid only had two. She doubted her own resolve to teach Raiden some magic.

"Okay, here it goes for whatever worth it is." Melinda put her hand on Raiden's chest. "Your heart is the source of the magic power you have. And the receptors in your body allow you to utilize that magic."

"What is the source of magic?" Raiden asked. "Just our hearts?"

"I don't know for certain, but the historians have written that it may be the God-weapons that are scattered around the worlds. But that's just a theory by historians. What today's mages believe is that we accumulate the energy available in the space where we are at the exact moment of our birth. So, the amount of energy we absorb at birth determines what kind of magic we have and how many aura lines generate from our heart." Melinda restricted herself to saying as few things as possible. She didn't want to overwhelm him with lots of information.

"So, the more magic around you, the more magic you can use? What's the use of aura lines, then?" Raiden asked.

"No, that's not the case, kid." She threw her hands in air. "It's a small thing. Okay, listen again." She paused, checking to be sure she had Raiden's full attention. "Magic is like cosmic energy, which is the same everywhere. Even dark mages use the same magic as us, but the nature of their magic is different than ours. It's the power in your heart and connecting aura lines that defines how much magic you can pull out of your surroundings and channel." There were other ways too, and magic could be improved slightly with magical artifacts, but Raiden didn't need to know that.

"Okay." Raiden seemed to have understood some but not everything. "Then what's the use of receptors?"

"Receptors are for initiation. Humans or even dark mages require receptors to turn their magic flow on. Remember, even you were initiated by a dark mage. I don't know why they initiated you at this age. It is normally done at the age of five. I have never heard of it being done on an adult like you before." She sighed at the thought of the pain this kid must have endured to go through initiation. These days, the kids were put under a complex anesthesia and then put through initiation. She knew it was way more painful than it appeared to be.

Raiden's face darkened. "I don't know their purpose, but I'm sure about one thing. No matter what, I will find my Anna and make them pay for it."

"Then you'd better learn to use magic. Your battle skills are nothing in front of the real magic, dark magic," Melinda said. She had faced a dark mage few a years back, and she didn't care for it to happen again.

Raiden nodded. Melinda wasn't sure if Raiden truly understood everything, but that was all she could explain without getting into too many nitty-gritty technical terms that could topple even experienced mages.

"How do we do it, then?" Raiden looked at his hands, like he was waiting for magic to emerge out of them automatically.

Melinda smiled at his childishness. "It won't work that way. If you want to cast a spell, you need to know how it feels inside your heart. Now close your eyes and touch my temple. I will cast a basic fireball and shoot it toward the sky."

If a caster wanted to let anyone feel his or her persona while casting magic, touching the temple worked pretty well, but the same method could let the next person creep into the caster's thoughts more than required. It didn't bother Melinda, though, as the process required a high-level mage to take advantage of the caster, and Raiden wasn't one.

She felt the warm sensation of his hand over her temple. Then she began conjuring a simple spell. She just had to think about pulling the magic out of her heart and convert the cosmic energy around her palm into fire.

Elemental magic was the basic magic every human in the world could use. Once a person turned eight, he would know his affinity toward one element, and by age ten he would start conjuring level two and beyond spells. Fire, Water, Air, Earth, and Lightning were the known elements that a human could use. Melinda didn't know what affinity Raiden possessed, or even if he possessed any, but she was trying to teach him how it felt to conjure magic. Once he knew the feeling, the rest should come easily.

Melinda watched Raiden carefully as his demeanor changed from a blank expression to one of realization. Did he feel something already? She thought so.

"Did you feel it?" she asked.

He nodded. "Let me try," he said and closed his eyes.

Melinda focused her magic meter on him, watching his magic lines light up as he tried to call upon his magic. For a moment, she thought she saw the lightest display of the line she had ever seen, but then it died, and nothing happened.

"I can't do this, I'm sorry." He pushed his hair back, appearing frustrated beyond her imagination.

"Don't worry, everything will be all right." She tried to give him hope that even she didn't have.

Chapter 10

VISAKA

"It's amazing, isn't it, Captain?" Bradok watched over her shoulder.

"It is." Visaka observed the circular shape of the weapon her radar had detected on the planet. It flowed with magic, more powerful than anything she had seen before.

Even their most robust magic meter couldn't measure it.

"I wonder who could have placed these on so many worlds scattered around our universe," Bradok said.

"It has to be God. That's why they call them God's weapons. But who knows what they really are." The weapon lay under mountains of dust and rock, because only nature could touch the weapons. Nobody had able to touch or analyze them before, and no one knew if the day would ever come that anyone could.

"Thousands have perished trying to touch it, and thousands will perish trying," Bradok added with a philosopher's touch.

The Axe of Thornos, another God weapon, lay on her planet under a pool of lava. That weapon was as big as a destroyer class warship. Someone had named the weapons scattered around hundreds of other worlds as well. But her ship's database didn't contain any name for this weapon. Was it because no one had ever seen it before?

Every ship built by humans had a sensor for such weapons, because if they accidentally landed too close to any one of them they would be instantly vaporized. Visaka wondered if a dark mage could get close to one of these weapons, or if they even had any on their side of the universe, the Quantum Zone.

She pulled her eyes away from the weapon. "Bradok, what's the status of the ship?"

"We are ready to depart," Bradok said.

"Re-check everything once more. Then we will jump through the portal." She had to visit the First Vessel and close the portal up again. She didn't know the reason behind keeping this planet hidden, but she would follow the protocol set by the first mage emperor.

"What are you going to do with the new guy? I think we can carry him with us. Cork mentioned he is not half bad." Bradok said.

"I'm not sure about him yet," Visaka replied. She hadn't given it much thought.

"Okay, I will re-check everything and initiate the jump. What would be our next course?"

"We are heading to the outer perimeter of Spectra 33 and bypass most worlds there. Then we will head to Archaic world Situla IV. We will see if we can get an oxygen module for our ship there, along with some missiles." Her ship needed an oxygen module, but having an old ship meant the parts were not easily available, at least not in the markets far away from the main trading planets. She could get a conversion specialist mage who could convert oxygen out of the other elements for her, but no one of that caliber would want to join a pirate ship. Failing that, her only option was an old mechanical converter that would prolong their space journey by a month's time. Right now, they had to visit an inhabited planet every fifteen days to replenish their oxygen supply.

Bradok closed the portal to Venus and started the procedure to run their hyperdrive at half-speed. Her ship could only run with half the speed of its original capacity for some reason. Neither she nor anyone aboard her ship could find out why; the controls remained locked. Maybe the ship was too old to use full power and the speed it travelled with was one fourth of what any newer ship could attain.

"Captain, hyperdrive is fully prepared. Ready to go on your cue. We will reach there in fifteen days time," Bradok said in a lenient tone. He had always been a loyal man to her, even before she became a pirate...

Visaka pushed her past away. She didn't need those thoughts. She was a free soul, and she was going to take advantage of that freedom.

Archaic planets didn't follow the mage emperor's rule, hence even the pirate ships could land there to trade. That was her only way to continue living.

"Let's go." She poured some of her magic into the hyperdrive connector and fired it up. She expected a smooth transition to a feeling of emptiness for a moment, and then they could continue doing their things while in hyperspace. But something went wrong, and a jerk to the ship shook them all. She watched Bradok fly upward and bang his head on the roof of the control bridge. The straps on her pilot chair had saved her ass.

She quickly glanced at the control display, but everything looked normal.

What was that? Is the hyperdrive failing? How? Bradok checked it before we left Venus.

"Bradok, are you all right?" She watched her engineering slowly float down toward floor; artificial gravity was kicking in.

"Yes, Captain. I will go and check the hyperdrive. For a moment I thought we broke our hyperdrive, but no warning sign has popped up on the screen." His brows lifted as he watched the display. "Wait... we never jumped into hyperspace at all."

"Ahh." That's why everything looked normal on Visaka's display. They were still in the dead zone, so there was nothing wrong with the ship's sensors. "Okay, go and check. We will jump again once you are done."

"Captain, something is wrong here. We are not in the dead zone anymore. We are on the edge of Spectra 1." Bradok turned his display unit in her direction. He was still shaking from the impact earlier.

"Not funny, Engineer. Spectra 1 is a month's distance from the dead zone, and even if we had the latest hyperdrive, we couldn't have reached it in less than fifteen days. It's impossible for our ship to travel that fast."

"I'm speaking the truth, Captain. We are just outside the perimeter of Spectra 1. Actually, we are at the perimeter of the Quantum Zone."

Visaka's eyes widened in alarm. How could they have jumped past the wards placed by the mage emperor's powerful magic? It was impossible. Even a dark mage could never get through the wards unless he found some crack in them, and the current mage emperor always made it a priority to fix those.

"Brandon, jump us out of here. Anywhere but here. Engage the hyperdrive at full power. I don't even care if we fall apart."

"We can't. There is a dark destroyer class ship coming at us." His voice cracked under the pressure.

"A dark destroyer?" Visaka's eyes darted to the display unit. A ship larger than anything she had seen before was looming over the edge of the Quantum Zone, and it was closing in on them rapidly. A destroyer was an army class ship that could withstand an attack of hundreds of fighters and come out victorious. There weren't many present in her king's army, because it required an enormous amount of magic to run, and only the King's close aides had that kind of magic. Her magic was feeble, human compared to that of the Gods. Even if she put her ship at full speed, the destroyer's missiles would tear her ship apart before she could jump back into hyperspace. Her scared mind couldn't understand what that ship was doing on the edge of the no-man's-zone between the human universe and the Quantum Zone.

"This must be a mistake. That ship can't be here for us." That was her last thought before she spotted hundreds of tiny ships pouring out of the destroyer. Every tiny ship was as big as her pirate ship. There was no way she could get out of this.

Chapter 11

RAIDEN

Raiden woke when the tip of his nose hit the cube's surface. He couldn't understand how he fell. The ship was supposed to be steady and smooth while traveling. *Are we in some kind of danger?* He rushed out of his cube, and saw Melinda running toward the control bridge. He instinctively followed her.

"This must be a mistake, that ship can't be here for us." He heard Visaka talking with Bradok, who stood in front of a control display.

Then he noticed hundreds of red dots were approaching their ship.

"What's happening, Captain? Why are there hundreds of red dots on the screen?" Raiden said.

"We are doomed. Dark fighter ships are on us." Visaka's tone cracked. For the first time, Raiden heard fear in her voice.

Melinda grabbed Visaka's shoulder. "But why? It doesn't make sense."

Visaka stared in Melinda's eyes. "I'm getting us out of here. We are jumping through the fourth dimension." Visaka's tone calmed down, but her face said it was just a calm before the storm. "Somehow, we jumped past the ward, creating a crack in it. We are going to use it to jump back."

Raiden was about to ask what that meant, but he stopped when he saw the mortified expression on Melinda's face.

"You can't do that. It's suicide," she said.

"What other choice do we have?" Visaka asked, tapping a button. A moment later, the control panel folded back into the desk below, and a surface came up with a blue mark embossed on a silver square.

Visaka touched that mark, and her body started glimmering with a blue sheen.

Raiden couldn't take his eyes off her. She looked like a divine angel. She began emitting blue light. Her power touched his heart, calling something inside him. Her body started radiating more and more light until he was blinded by it.

Then everything around them went dark. Dark shadows concealed everything on the ship. The darkness started absorbing the magic from everyone around him. First Melinda fell to the floor, and then Bradok fell. Finally, the light coming out of Visaka vanished in that darkness, too. He wanted to reach them and stop that dark shadow. He was about to take a step forward when he heard Anna's voice.

"Come to me, my love. I'm waiting for you."

"Anna!" He tried to look for her, but everything was so dark that he couldn't spot her. But he was sure she had called him from the darkness.

As quickly as the darkness appeared, it vanished too. Everything was clear around him again, but Visaka and her crew lay on the ground, unconscious. White foam was coming out of Visaka's mouth.

I need to get her to the medical bay.

Raiden knelt before her and lifted her up. She was lighter than he expected. He ran through the ship's long corridor to reach the medical bay. The moment he put her down on the berth, the ship's autonomous medical AI started scanning her body. His muscles remained tense as the scan took place. His heartbeat rose as the minutes passed and the AI scanned her body.

Five minutes passed, and the display showed the result. It was all green, and he assumed that meant everything was all right with her body. But Visaka was still unconscious, her face pure white, like she had just lost every ounce of magical energy from her body.

"I will put her under medication now." The autonomous bot told him after another ten minutes of scans.

"Do you think she's all right?" he asked.

"Yes, her physical condition is excellent, but her magical energy is completely drained. Hence, she is unconscious. I will put her to sleep, and when she wakes she will feel better," the bot replied in a mechanical voice.

"Thank you, Mr. Bot," he said.

"My name is TDK 143, and I don't need to be thanked for doing my job."

"Anyway, thanks." Raiden turned back, remembering Melinda and Bradok had fallen too. He quickly moved through corridor after corridor before he spotted them coming toward the medical bay.

"Is she all right?" Melinda asked as soon as she spotted him. "I still don't believe she pulled that off." She was sweating.

"The bot said she'll be all right after few hours of sleep. What did she do? Did you lose your magical energy too?" Raiden asked.

Bradok answered this time. "She transmitted us through the fourth dimension. We should be thankful that we didn't end up inside the heart of the Quantum Zone, or worse. She could be dead from exhaustion."

"But we can't forget that she saved our life from those fighter ships," Melinda said. "Let's just be happy that everyone is safe and she is not dead after making such a foolish decision."

"What are you talking about? What is this Quantum Zone?" Raiden asked.

"Nothing that concerns you. Thanks for taking her to the medical bay in time," Melinda answered coldly.

"Why didn't Raiden suffer any damage from the jump?" Bradok asked. "Every mage loses lots of magic when they jump through Quantum Zone."

"He doesn't have magic. Maybe that's why," Melinda said.

Lonely thoughts filled Raiden's heart. Reality sunk in. He was the only one without magic in the whole universe. He had to live with that and still save his Anna.

Can I really do this?

Chapter 12

ANNA

Anna stared at her master through the display.

"Master, I sensed them in the dark dimension. They passed through it briefly."

Her master regarded her with wary eyes. His ocular powers pierced her heart from a few light years' distance.

"I know. I have reports. I risked a war to get that ship, yet it vanished before my eyes. She used forbidden magic to travel through the dark dimension. I was so close to having that ship back." He grabbed a mage standing next to him and crushed his skull with bare hands.

"Why waste a mage, Master?" Anna asked.

"He led the assault on her ship, and even with a destroyer class, he failed."

Her master was angry, but she knew what would calm him down. "I'll get him to bring that ship to us. He listened to me. He reacted to my voice. He was in love with me for ten years, and he'll come back to me soon." She was determined to have Raiden back at her side, and then she would serve the ship to her master.

"I don't like failures, Magita," he groaned.

"I won't fail you, Master." Her master had renamed her after she'd turned out to be a true and powerful dark mage. She was nothing before meeting him, and now she understood the power pulsing through her body. Now she could do anything and everything she had ever dreamed of.

"Hone your skills, and you may be my ultimate pawn when the time comes." Her master disconnected the magic link he had formed with void magic, something which was only possible for his kind. For a mere mage like her, that was an impossible feat.

She concentrated on her magic again, trying to sense Raiden, but he was gone, disappeared from the dark dimension. Raiden was an essential element in the task given by her master, and she had faint memories of him being with her forever before she became the all-powerful Magita. When she had sensed Raiden inside the dark dimension, she had quickly reached out to him: a plan had formed inside her mind, a plan that would gain her more power and loyalty in her master's eyes.

She wondered if it was Raiden who'd transported his ship through the dark dimension. Had he gained that much power in such a short time? No, that wasn't possible. He didn't have a master like hers to teach him, to hone his magic. She doubted Raiden would attain power like hers anytime soon, because his initiation failed miserably. If Raiden had somehow attained the power she thought of, she wanted him on her side. With him, she would win this war and emerge even stronger than anyone she had ever known.

Chapter 13

RAIDEN

The next day Raiden spent most of his time talking with Melinda and watching over the captain. He felt gratitude toward the captain for saving him and for letting him live on the ship. Attending to her was the least he could do to show that gratitude. Through this task, he learned lots of information about the new world that had been built in the last thousand years by talking with Melinda.

"Two thousand years. I feel old, too old, but still too naive for all of this," Raiden said. Melinda had told him that an average mage lived almost two hundred years, a result of mixing science and magic together. A few mages, like the mage emperor, lived up to three hundred years. The current mage emperor of the Spectra system was one hundred years old. In another hundred years, the search for the next mage emperor would begin. All of the mage kings of the Spectra system were in the running. "Everything I knew has changed. People, politics, everything. I feel so out of place."

"You are just older than twenty, right?" Melinda asked.

"Twenty-six, in Earth years. I was in my prime back on Earth, but I guess I'm a child in this new era of mages." He paused to gather his words. "I wonder if I'll also live two hundred years. Maybe not. I don't have any magic like you guys."

What about Anna? Would she live that long too? Thought of humans living two hundred years meant he could spend lots of years with his love... if he ever got her back. Sadness crawled inside his mind. He was losing a little more hope every day.

"I don't know. You are a rare case, among the rarest we have in our universe. But don't worry, even without magic you would live at least a hundred years in your prime. Never forget that we have equally powerful science. Without science, magic is nothing."

Melinda tried hard, but she failed to lighten any hope in Raiden's heart. From the moment he understood that he held no magic and couldn't even use other's magic in the suit, loneliness had filled his mind.

"So, this mage king or emperor, how much magic does he or she have?" Raiden asked curiously.

"I guess too much for a magic meter to measure. They even possess the ancient artifacts called charms. Those charms, or words of magic, enhance their abilities manyfold."

"Was he so powerful from birth? Like the son or daughter of an earlier king or something?" Raiden wondered if the new system was democratic or military based.

"Something like that. But even being a son or daughter of the king doesn't make you powerful. Only few of the king's kids possesses compatible magic powers. Once their magical powers are determined, they undergo harsh training on the Mage emperor's planet—Sutra—where he himself chooses a few worthy to serve from each Spectra world. These mages go back to their own Spectra systems and serve people to win their hearts.

Finally, they participate in a worldwide election, and we get a new king. So, if you calculate all of this, every king rules Spectra around 110 years before the people chose a new king." Melinda paused to check on Visaka, who had started making some movements. "I think she is about to wake up."

Raiden looked at the captain. She was a young lady and appeared to be in her twenties, but he couldn't trust his guts this time. She could be seventy years old. But right the, she looked like a twenty year old girl sleeping like a baby. Her face had always been tense, but in sleep she remained peaceful.

Visaka moved a bit, and then her eyes fluttered open. She stiffened when she spotted Raiden but eased instantly as her eyes darted to Melinda.

"Where am I?" she asked.

"Captain you are in the medical bay." The bot, TDK 143 walked to her.

"Thanks, for taking care of me." Visaka looked at Melinda with smiling eyes. "I must have collapsed. I'm still not used to the jump through the fourth dimension."

"Say thanks to this kid here who bought you here in time. We were all down on the ground with you, but you were in the worst shape. I never thought you would try that jump so suddenly."

"Dire situation, dire measures. Anyway, where are we now? I hadn't thought about a place when I pulled us through the fourth dimension," Visaka said.

"We are near the Archaic planets. I guess you were thinking about them when you triggered the jump," Melinda said.

"Yes, that was the initial plan. But I don't know how we ended up at the perimeter of Spectra 1 earlier. We couldn't theoretically do that." Visaka's face turned hard.

"Don't worry about it right now. We are safe here, and we should focus on the next plan. Bradok says we are stranded here for few more days, as our hyperdrive suffered some damage during that jump." Melinda said.

"Hmm." Visaka closed her eyes and went back to her thoughts.

Raiden observed her closely. She was one heck of a strong woman.

"Melinda." The comm in the medical bay came to life. It was Bradok, and he sounded urgent.

"Bradok, it's Visaka, tell me what happened." The captain spoke instead.

"Captain, you are back. Good. We have incoming. Two pirate ships are about to enter our hyper-jump perimeter, and I don't think they have good intentions," Bradok said.

"What's their class?" Visaka asked.

"Fighter class, same as us. But they are the latest Archaic builds, and our hyperdrive is still offline."

"We can fly around, and you have the best cadet from the flying academy of mages as your captain." A smile lit up Visaka's face. "It's action time." She jumped down from the berth.

"But, Visaka, your magic, it's not replenished yet," Melinda said, concern in her voice.

"I don't need magic to outclass these fighters. My flying skills are enough for them." Visaka moved out the door toward the control bridge. She paused for a moment. "Thanks, newbie. Appreciate your help."

Raiden followed her to the control bridge with a smile on his face. It felt good to be in the Captain's good graces. Maybe he could convince her to help him find Anna.

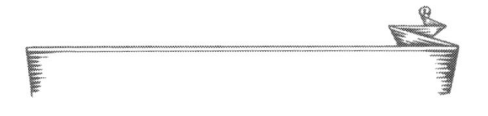

Chapter 14

RAIDEN

"Welcome back, Captain." Bradok smiled at the Captain when they entered the control bridge.

Visaka took charge of the control panel.

Raiden searched for anything he could help with, but he could do nothing but stand there watching. A display panel next to him showed two red dots closing on their ship.

Two pirate ships. What will she do now? He focused on the captain's actions.

"Bradok, have our missiles ready in case of a final push," Visaka said.

"But Captain, we only have four left," Bradok said.

"I know. I'm not planning to use them all. Just be ready." Visaka tapped a button on the screen, and a few threads came out of the control panel and pierced four black dots just below her neck.

"What's that?" Raiden looked at Melinda, who stood next to him, looking at his display.

"Oh, that?" She glanced at Visaka, whose chair had flattened out. A joystick-like control had emerged from the roof of the control bridge as well. "It's a magic human interface used to redirect magic to the receivers in the ship. It's useful for mages like us to defend the ships. It amplifies our magic, so we can take down other ships."

"What about the dots under her skin? That must be painful."

"Those are created for jumpers when they are initiated in their childhood. Visaka is the best jumper her world has seen in ages." Melinda's face lit with pride.

Raiden would have asked more, but then he saw Visaka engage the controls. As she pushed the joystick-like controls, their ship jolted forward. "Oh, wow. This is like playing a simulator game."

"A game? Do you really think this is a game, kid?" Melinda raised her brows. "A single wrong move and we will be dead."

"No, no. It's not…" He grabbed his chair tightly as the ship rotated ninety degrees to avoid an incoming missile.

"Where the hell did that come from?" Raiden shouted, strapping himself into the chair.

"It was cloaked with an invisibility spell by the enemy mage. They must have a level four jump mage, too," Melinda said.

Raiden wondered about the levels and made a note to ask about it later. Right now, he wanted to observe the captain.

Visaka directed their ship toward one of the pirate ships. Raiden gripped the chair handles as he saw the ship in real time on the display. It was bigger than theirs and looked brand new. The ship was triangular with a large ring rotating around the base vertices. A huge cannon was attached to the ship's upper surface, and a man in some kind of tech suit stood behind it. Raiden guessed he was the one firing missiles.

Visaka was doing nothing but rotating their ship at crazy speeds to avoid incoming missiles.

"What's that man doing behind the cannon?" Raiden asked. "I thought a mage could fire a magical missile from the control bridge. Didn't Bradok do that?"

"Only if the ship's jumper mage can direct his magic to the weapon system. If the ship's jumper mage can't do that, then they have to use the interface directly mounted on the spellcannon," Melinda said.

Raiden suddenly understood how important Visaka was and what an important job she did on the ship. Her eyes were closed, but her face was tight and sharp. She was giving a lot to the ship even when her magic wasn't replenished.

Raiden pitied the captain and wondered if anyone else could help her.

"She's one of the toughest women I've ever seen," he muttered to himself. He had known many women in the military who were tough like steel, and they could do things a man couldn't, but flying a spaceship like this... he bet even the best of men from this new world couldn't do that.

Apparently, the enemy ship's pilot couldn't match Visaka's skills, so when she directed *Challenger* toward the enemy ship he turned back to flee, which stopped their missile attacks.

"Bradok, be ready with the first missile. It has to be close range. We are destroying this one," Visaka commanded, even with her eyes closed.

"Aye, aye, Captain." The engineer tapped at the controls.

The display in front of Raiden showed an outside view of their ship. A turret slowly emerged from their ship, and a missile was mounted on it. Bradok pressed his hand to the control panel, and Raiden thought he saw a yellow light pass from Bradok's hands into the control panel. A moment later, yellow light covered the missile displayed on his screen.

"Is that Bradok's magic covering the missile?" he asked.

"Yes, fire magic," Melinda said.

Then Raiden saw something that he never thought he would see in his whole life. The captain thrust their ship toward the fleeing ship at full speed. *Challenger* closed on the enemy ship too fast for it to avoid. Just as he braced for impact, Visaka pulled the ship up and they crossed over the enemy ship with only a few meters between them.

"Now," Visaka commanded.

Bradok fired the missile. The missile hit the ship, and fire incinerated the ship in a blaze. In less than a second, no trace of the enemy ship remained, just a blank space.

"Wow, that was crazy," Raiden muttered.

"That was nothing. I've seen her do crazier things than this. Didn't I say she was the best jumper in the whole academy?" Melinda smiled.

"Bradok, be ready with the next one," Visaka said. "But don't put fire magic in it. We are going to hit their hyperdrive. I want that ship alive. We need to raid that ship."

"Aye, aye, Captain," the engineer replied.

"Raid?" Raiden rolled his eyes.

"Yes. We are pirates, after all." Melinda sighed quietly. She didn't look happy about it.

Bradok prepared the next missile while Visaka maneuvered the ship toward the second ship.

Raiden focused his display unit on the second ship, which was already firing many more missiles than the first ship had fired. He guessed they were going all out, as they'd just seen how crazy Visaka was.

Visaka dodged these missiles easily, but then she faced a multi-turret missile, which was a cluster of missiles that broke into hundreds of small ones when it was just few kilometers away from their ship.

Raiden's heart pumped faster. He couldn't guess what Visaka would do now. She could easily get the ship away from earlier missiles because they were fewer in number, but what about these hundred missiles spread across a few kilometers, closing in on them rapidly? What would she do? His mind went numb as the missiles drew closer to their ship.

Chapter 15

MELINDA

Melinda stared at the display as the missiles closed in. She knew Visaka would have some plan or thought about how to avoid these small, magic-filled missiles. This second ship was doing good, and they had reacted to the situation well. They seemed to have a powerful mage. She could see the missiles cloaked in fire magic. Maybe they were not as powerful as what Bradok had used, but when you had hundreds of small ones, the effect could still be devastating.

What will do you now, princess?

Visaka applied the front thrusters and upper thrusters at the same time, and the ship started dropping down like a stone. The missiles didn't stop, though. They followed. They were guided magic missiles.

"Cork, I need some of your lightning magic. I'm going to transport our ship on top of that ship," Visaka said.

"But you are out of magic! You can't pull off that spell with the whole ship." The captain was crazy. Transportation magic was Cork's specialty, but Visaka didn't have enough energy left in herself to divert Cork's spell to the ship.

"Don't worry, I have just enough," Visaka said. "Cork, do it now."

Melinda looked at Cork, who was eating something while watching the fight. He was always the reckless one among them all. He cursed more than he breathed, and he ate more than he cursed.

"What about the missiles?" Melinda asked.

"I have an idea, but first we need to incapacitate that ship," Visaka said.

Cork jumped to his feet and left his food on the control panel's display. Melinda wanted to warn him not to do that, but saving their ass was more important. Cork poured his magic into the control panel, and the next moment their ship vanished and re-appeared on top of the enemy ship.

"Bradok, fire," Visaka ordered.

Bradok triggered the missiles, this time without any magic. The missiles hit the pirate ship's hyperdrive, disabling the enemy ship without damaging it too much.

"Melinda, can you put a shield spell around the ship?" Visaka asked. "We have to cover both ships now. We don't want the pirate ship to be damaged by their own missiles. We have work for it."

Melinda looked at Visaka. Her head was fully covered in sweat, and her breathing had become disruptive. She looked completely drained, but somehow she was still holding it together.

Some day you are going to regret this, kid.

Visaka cared for others, and that's why she always put her life on the line to save her crew. If only her father, King of Spectra 33, understood her faith and value. She would have been an excellent leader by now. Melinda shook her head. It wasn't the time for grieving for the past. They had a ship to protect.

Melinda poured her magic into the system and formed a defensive fire shield around *Challenger* and the remaining pirate ship. The missiles closed in and started hitting the shield. It wasn't a big task for her to create that shield, but it was a big task for Visaka to keep Melinda's magic flowing through the ship's hull. While connected to the ship, she felt Visaka's magic waning a couple of times, resulting in missiles hitting their ship, damaging parts of it. But each time, Visaka channeled more magic, recovering the shield to protect them from the next batch of missiles.

The barrage continued for couple of minutes, then stopped. Melinda watched the drained Visaka almost lose her grip on the chair as the time passed, but she couldn't do anything. Raiden was the first one to reach out to Visaka and help her remain on her chair when the lasts of the missiles hit.

The interface retracted when Visaka couldn't support it anymore. Foam had started coming out of her mouth. Raiden was quick to pull her out of the chair and make a run for the medical bay. She had once again put her life in danger.

Melinda stared at the pilot's chair with teary eyes. She felt helpless and frustrated because she couldn't help her princess. She remembered when Visaka was a child, she used to overdo things and fall over in exhaustion, and Melinda had to carry her back to palace. Now she had responsibilities when the captain was knocked out. She had to march her mages and raid the pirate ship, otherwise Visaka's sacrifice would be wasted.

"Raiden, come back to the control bridge once you put the captain under the supervision of the medical bot," Melinda ordered him over the comms.

"What now?" Cork asked as he picked his sandwich back up.

"We are going to raid the ship. Prepare to dock, put the ship on autopilot, and the four of us will make our way onto the pirate ship."

"We four? Do you want to take the newbie as well?" Cork asked.

"He is good in hand-to-hand combat. We should take him with us. Find out if he can use some marine weapon or give him your axe." Melinda remembered the way Raiden fought with the creature back on Venus. "He has proved he can use it."

Chapter 16

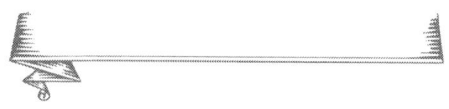

RAIDEN

Raiden attended to Visaka with care. She was down again due to the exhaustion of the space battle. His respect for her grew tenfold when he saw her taking on the two pirate ships alone. She was one hell of a woman.

The new world he was seeing hadn't been easy for him. So many things had happened after he woke up in that dark corridor. His love, Anna, had been tortured and then kidnapped. He still didn't know how to rescue her. Then he learned about magic, which wasn't useful to him at all. Then he found out about what happened to Earth, and the new regime of mages. He lost sleep, thinking he didn't really belong in this future.

The events of the day led him to ponder that again. He'd seen a space battle with three pirate ships taking on each other for blood. He wasn't afraid of blood. In fact, he had killed many people in Afghanistan. He was a soldier for years, and he ran covert operations in many middle eastern countries fighting against terrorism. Killing wasn't new to him, but at the end of the day, it needed to have a purpose. When he heard Melinda calling the crew pirates, he doubted their resolve.

He sighed as Visaka twisted on the medical berth. TDK 143 continued its scans.

Raiden lapsed into thoughts of life on earth. He was a soldier for many years, but three years back he'd left the military for Anna and joined a security agency to provide protection to important people. He still remembered the night he'd bought a ring for Anna. The next day, he'd proposed her. She'd said yes, and they'd spent the night cuddling each other, discussing their future, naming their future kids. He'd fallen asleep with a smile that night, only to wake up to this nightmare.

He needed a drink. If only these magicians could conjure alcohol out of thin air. He sighed.

Visaka shifted, and he lost his train of thought again.

Cork walked into the medical bay. "Newbie, Melinda is calling you."

"For what?"

"We are going to raid the pirate ship. And we already know that you can fight." Cork smirked at him. Though he had become a bit warmer toward Raiden, he still had his quirkiness intact.

"I dunno, Cork." Raiden struggled to put his thoughts into words. "Maybe I'm not supposed to come with you guys. I'm not a pirate, and I dunno. I'm just not comfortable raiding a ship for personal gain."

Cork's eyes turned red in response to the judgment passed on him. "What the fuck? You are on a pirate ship, pig, so believe it or not, that makes you a pirate too. And we are not raiding a civilian ship or a merchant ship. We are raiding a damn fucking pirate ship which would have killed us if we hadn't defeated them."

Raiden looked at Cork without knowing what to answer. "Maybe I should stay here and look after the captain. I've got a feeling she needs me."

"Fine with me. Tuck your head all you want in your own ass. The three of us are enough for a puny pirate ship." Cork gave him a stern look and walked away.

"I'm sorry Captain, but I did what I thought was right," Raiden muttered, looking at Visaka. She was still sleeping like a child.

Chapter 17

VISAKA

When Visaka opened her eyes, she found Raiden talking with the medical bot.

How could he talk with a bot?

She felt a twinge of compassion for this man. He was doing better than she'd expected. When they had first met, he was nothing but a threat to them. He'd been initiated by a dark mage, and they didn't know the extent of the corruption he had inherited from the initiation ritual, but in the end he turned out to be a rare non-magical human. She tried to remember the last time she'd heard about someone like him in her whole lifetime. It was never, because even the non-magic users her world had could perform some basic form of magic. They were called non-magical people because they couldn't conjure any level two spell, but they could perform level one spells with some practice and live a normal life. Raiden was different, and whatever path he chose would be difficult. She felt for him. If she could help him somehow, she would be happy to do it.

"How are you feeling, Captain?" Raiden asked as he noticed Visaka staring at him.

"You can call me Visaka when it's just the two of us. And I'm better right now. How did the mission go?"

"I didn't go, but the others are back and resting in their cubes."

"Hmm." Visaka wondered why he hadn't gone with the others. Maybe he had his own reasons.

"Can I ask you something, Captain?" Raiden looked in her eyes.

"Go ahead," she said, wondering what he would he ask.

"When did you chose to become a pirate? And why? I've only known you for few days, but your ethics seem way better than a pirate's. It doesn't seem like your style." He pushed his hair back. "You know what I mean, right?"

"A pirate?" When had she chosen to become one? Heck, she'd had no other choice but to live as pirate to survive. But when did she really choose to be a pirate, and act like one? She couldn't answer that question. It had its own story, but the result was the same: she was a pirate, destroying other pirate ships for resources and gold.

Maybe it all started with your death, Victor, my brother.

"Yes, a pirate." Raiden's eyes bore into hers.

"Why do you want to know that? And why didn't you join the mission with others?" Knowing his reason was essential before she could tell him why she became pirate. How much longer could she hide her betrayal to her world, to her king, to her father? Everyone aboard the ship knew it, and some day Raiden would hear it from the others, and then he would judge her without knowing her side of the story. Many had done that before. Even her father and her love, Richard, judged her based on that video footage. Why would this stranger be different than her blood bonds?

"Maybe I'm not ready for this. I'm not a mage or a pirate. It doesn't suit me," Raiden said, looking away.

So this man was like the others, judging the profession she was playing at by the name of it.

"What do you want to do with your life, then?" She had hoped that Raiden would join her crusade, whatever it was, and live with her party of lone wolves. When was the last time her wish had come true?

"I want to find Anna, my love. I was hoping you would help me."

"Why would I do that?" She couldn't believe he was hoping for help from her when he totally refused to join her team on the mission. Heat flashed through her cheeks. Raiden reminded her of everyone that had judged her without asking her side of the story and then called her a traitor. Raiden was also a selfish man to judge her by her profession. She might have looted and killed people, but she made sure she only attacked pirate ships. If she was still in her father's army and killed a few pirates, these people would have treated her like a hero. Instead, they called her a lowly traitor. Raiden's display of helpfulness in the last battle was a mere coincidence. She had again failed to understand a man.

"I don't know," he said. "I just want to save my love, at any cost. Even if that means I have to take on the dark mages by myself." Raiden's eyes filled with determination.

Reality sunk in her mind. He was a pawn of fate, too. If she was right, Anna would have been converted by now, and there was little hope that she could be saved anymore. Even if Visaka decided to help him, there was no way they could snatch Anna back from the heart of the Quantum Zone. That was off-limits for any human mage.

"The most I can do is to drop you on some Archaic world, and you can choose your own path from there." Visaka knew she was breaking his heart, but she had no other option.

Raiden's eyes fell. She could see his soul getting crushed through his eyes. He looked at her once and then left the medical bay.

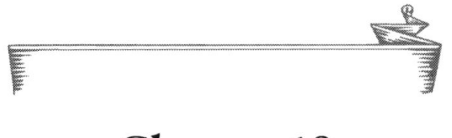

Chapter 18

ANNA

Anna opened her eyes when she felt her master's overwhelming presence. His magic reached out to her even before he emerged from the dark dimension. She wondered what it would take to become as powerful as he was in her own lifetime. She pushed that thought away and bowed as he stepped through the portal.

"Master Vakoxir, what brings you here?" she asked without looking at him. He was the king of who knew how many worlds and only reported to the mighty one, the dark God she'd only heard rumors about. She had a feeling that soon she would be seeing that God, and that would change her life forever.

"Yes, my prodigy, I wanted to see how much you have progressed." Vakoxir's voice echoed in the mediation room she was practicing her magic in.

"I could have come to you, master," she replied in faint voice. Her ambitions were higher, but she had to be careful not to insult him in any way.

"Show me what you can do," he said and waved his hands. Two swarns appeared out of thin air. "These are your opponents."

The swarns unsheathed their swords.

Puny weapons.

"Don't be deceived by their puny weapons. These weapons are made from iron cast in the breath of a God. That gives them immense power," her master said.

She looked at them with fresh eyes. A red glaze oozed out of their swords. She remembered blood magic and how it worked. If these swords touched her blood somehow, her body would be bound to the wielder of the magic. There was no way she could engage them in close combat. She had to stick with elemental magic.

One of the swarn jumped in the air and swung his sword above his head to strike her down. The air around her heated as he closed in on her with sheer force and intent to kill.

She smiled at him. The sword closed the distance between them, but before it could land, she vanished inside the ground below her. A moment later, her hands emerged from the ground and wrapped around the swarn's legs, pulling him down. The swarn snarled viciously and tried to slice her hands, but his sword couldn't hit her. In a matter of seconds, he was pulled deep underground, the ground above him smooth and even, like nothing happened.

The second swarn watched with focused eyes. He pushed his wings out and flew up in the air, perhaps thinking that touching the ground would mean a similar end for him.

Anna emerged out of the ground and watched him fly around her. She was still smiling. Her magic was just getting warmed up. She had already admitted to herself, thousands of times, that this feeling the magic inside her was the best thing that had ever happened to her. She loved that feeling so much that she needed more, and her master was going to provide her that power.

The swarn dashed toward her, his sword poised to attack. He swung when he got closer to Anna, but his sword passed through her body without hurting her as if it moved through her shadow. He retreated, hesitation in his posture, then darted to her again, this time dancing his sword in front of him. The result was the same. The thrust went through her without even touching her. He looked around, searching for some explanation.

She smiled again, and this time she shot a cone of stone out of her hand. She was happy how her earth magic was turning out.

The swarn ducked the stone cone and darted at her, and again his sword passed through her body. He retreated again, eyes watching her every movement.

Anna vanished back into the ground. Earth, or any stable surface, reacted to her magic however she wanted. She was the mage of Earth, a dark mage specializing in earth magic. But she wasn't just that. She was much more than that. She had access to the dark dimension like she owned it, and she was going to use that power to kill this creature. When she vanished into the ground, she moved into the dark dimension and stepped out just behind the swarn.

Anna pushed her hand on the back of the swarn's armor and hit him with a level two stone cone. The cone pierced his body and shattered, leaving a hole in his body. The swarn fell.

Anna drifted down and kneeled in front of her master. He smiled at her.

Chapter 19

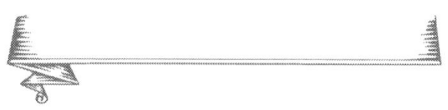

RAIDEN

Raiden rested his head on his knees while he thought about his next move. Actually, he didn't have a clue what he was going to do next. He had no magic. He didn't know how this new world worked, and his Anna had been kidnapped by the worst criminals of this world. He didn't even know how to find her in the first place. Now his only hope, the brave captain, had said that she would drop him on a neutral planet to find his own way.

What should I do now, Lord?

For the first time in his life, he felt powerless. He thought about his hardships on planet Earth, and he had gone through the worst. One time, he was captured by five terrorists and tortured a lot, but even then, he didn't feel powerless like he felt now.

"Hey, Raiden, what are you thinking about?" Melinda's voice echoed in his cube.

He opened his eyes to find her smiling at him. Was she teasing him because he just got kicked out of the ship by the captain?

"What do you want?" He was in no mood to talk to her right now. He needed time to think about his situation and find a way out of this impossible situation. Talking with Melinda wasn't going to help him find his Anna.

"I'm here to help you." She grabbed the only stool present in his cube.

"Are you here to tell me about the planet you're going to drop me on to die?" he asked with a smug look on his face.

"No, I'm not here to tell you that. I want to help you, kid."

"Why would you do that? I said no to your pirate mission, and now your captain wants to get rid of me. I understand she's a pirate, but does that mean she doesn't have a heart?" Raiden's voice was shrill. He was pissed off, and he was unloading on the first person he met after the discussion with the captain.

"Do you really think she is heartless?" Melinda's eyes burned like fire. He'd clearly struck a nerve. "If you had known her when she was a princ—" She looked away.

"When she was what? She's nothing but a pirate, and she kills people for money. That's what she is," Raiden continued, unable to stop himself. Even he couldn't believe he had this much hatred filling his heart.

Melinda stood up and conjured a fireball out of her hand. She lunged forward and held her spell next to Raiden's eyes. "One more word, and you will lose your whole head. You don't get to say a single word against her." Her fiery eyes were filled with craziness.

Heat from the spell warmed Raiden's face. He backed down. "I'm sorry." It was foolishness to even think she didn't mean what she said.

Raiden's fist clenched and hit wall behind him as Melinda moved away. That's the only thing he could do without any magic or powers. He was nothing in this world, and still he thought he could carve his way out of this situation. How foolish he could be?

"Calm down, kid. Hitting the wall isn't going to give you anything but more frustration." Melinda's voice had returned to normal.

"What should I do? How can I gain power? How can I save my love without magic? Even if I learn magic, is it possible to get her back from the dark mages you guys are so afraid of?"

"Who said we are afraid of them? We are not. Our first emperor, George, placed a ward so powerful around our galaxy that not even a bender class dark mage can enter inside it. It even breaks the lines of the fourth dimension, so no one can jump from the Quantum Zone into our side of the galaxy." Melinda's voice was filled with pride.

"So, this emperor, can he help me get back my Anna?" Raiden's eyes filled with hope, a hope he hadn't felt for so many days.

"He can't. He is dead. The current emperor can, but he won't," Melinda said.

"But why? If he's so strong, then he can easily get my Anna back. Then I'll move to some distant planet where these dark mages can't reach me and live my life happily ever after."

"Do you really think that an emperor who looks after all of humanity would listen to a mere human like you and help?" She giggled.

"He should, if he's so powerful," Raiden said, but he too began to recognize his own folly.

"Even if he decides to help a common citizen, why would he help a pirate like you? You are part of Visaka's crew, and that makes you a pirate, my friend." She looked away, "Besides, he is always so busy that he doesn't even have time for me." She paused. "Or anyone, I meant to say."

"There has to be a way out of this. Some magic or some trick I can use to call her back, or something like Visaka did. Maybe I can go through that fourth dimension and snatch her from the dark mages. That should be possible, shouldn't it?" Raiden threw some ideas on the table.

"No one can do that, other than a jumper class mage like Visaka. And you have seen what happened to her when she did that last time. She almost died." Melinda said. "Anyway, not all ships have the power rune to pull that off. We have a kind of special ship in our hands, so Visaka's able to do it."

"But she didn't die, did she? Is she the strongest mage you've ever met?" Raiden asked.

"No, not by a long shot. Any Spectra king's navy would have hundreds of stronger mages than her when it comes to sheer power, but there are not many jumper class mages better than her. Every jumper class mage in our universe is assigned to some navy ship, so finding one without any connection to the king is impossible."

"Come on, there has to be something out there that can help me in this."

Melinda paused for a brief moment, giving Raiden a considering look.

"You have an idea, don't you? Please tell me. If magic exists in this universe, there has to be something that can help me get Anna back."

"What if that thing will cost you your life?" Melinda asked. "No, we can't do that. Rumors are that it takes a specialized mage to wield that crystal. You don't even have basic magic. The crystal will eat your magic completely."

"What crystal?" A hope welled inside him again.

"It's a dark crystal, said to be carved from the mountain of the dark God's home planet. It possesses the dark magic capable of letting someone travel through the fourth dimension without being a jumper class mage. As you know, the dark dimension affects mages in the very worst manner." Her shoulders sagged. "It's not a path I want you to go on."

"But that dimension, or whatever it is, didn't affect me at all. Maybe being without magic helped me in that."

"Even if you get your hands on the crystal, how are you going to use it? You don't have magic to channel into the crystal. It's useless to you, Raiden."

"I don't know, but I'm sure we'll find some way out of this." Raiden smiled at Melinda. "Tell me where to find this crystal."

"If you want to get one, we are going in the right direction. Visaka is taking us to Situla IV, an Archaic world, to trade some tech equipment, and I know a black market trader who may know where we can get this crystal."

For the first time in many days, Raiden didn't feel helpless. There was something he could do to save Anna. Now he just had to find a way to use the crystal without magic.

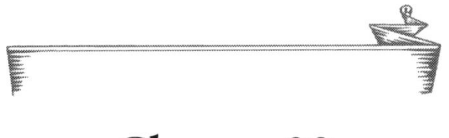

Chapter 20

VISAKA

Visaka called everyone—Melinda, Bradok, and Cork—to the control bridge. Most ships had marines on them too, low magic users who could use Type Three spell'O'armor and perform ship maintenance. Her ship didn't have any marines. Why would anyone join her pirate ship? It was just as well; she didn't trust others very much. Melinda had been with her since childhood, and Bradok had been with her since her academic years, so they both had her trust. She didn't know Cork much, but he was Bradok's brother and that was enough for her to trust him.

Raiden followed the others onto the control bridge. Visaka welcomed him with a cocked brow, unsure what was he doing there. He'd made it clear that he didn't want to have anything to do with pirates, but he was there for the briefing anyway.

Whatever. Who cares?

"Team, we are going to land on Situla IV in two days' time, so I wanted to give a piece of advice to you all. Situla IV is a military trading center of the Archaic system, and they have a very strict law against using magic on the streets. Even showing magic on the streets is treated as a criminal offense. If spotted, the accused will be given severe punishment. So, my advice to you is to keep your magic inside, and if required, use the mechanical weapons." She paused for a moment and stared at Raiden, who was carefully listening to every word she said. "Not that I foresee any trouble, as the planetary police force is pretty good at keeping trouble in check, but still I wouldn't want to lose a crew member for a foolish reason."

"What about the gold, Captain? Can we buy some things? A frigging sweetmeats girl is what I want." Cork seemed excited by the idea of landing on an inhabited planet after so long out in space.

Visaka thought back. When was the last time they'd landed on a trading planet? It'd been nearly six months. They'd made sure to land now and then to replenish their oxygen supplies, but those planets provided little in the sense of trading, so no one left the ship.

Bradok raised his voice. "Language, brother."

"Go ahead, Sergeant," Visaka said. "You're all getting extra gold for the success of the last mission. So, enjoy. We will be docked for four days." She smiled, knowing Cork could be a jerk sometimes, but she didn't care as long as he stayed away from the ladies on the ship.

"How much are you left with, from Titan?" Melinda whispered.

"Not much, but enough to buy some tech for this aging ship," Visaka said. She never used the gold she stole from other pirate ships. It was stolen from people around the universe, directly or indirectly, so she always made sure that she used the gold she carried with her when she left Titan. Her reserves were draining with every trading trip she made, and she had to gain some legitimate gold soon, or she would be in trouble. It was already hard to keep herself away from the Royal Navy, and she didn't need any more trouble.

Melinda and Bradok left, leaving Raiden and Cork, who was holding a kind of suit pack in his hands.

"Speak up, Raiden. I thought you wouldn't want to participate in any mission we pirates undertake." Her words pierced his subtle eyes, but that was her aim.

"I'm sorry if I hurt you, Captain, but I was hoping I could visit Situla IV as well. I don't know anything about the universe, and if I have go it alone I need to learn more about it."

"No, it would be too dangerous for you leave the ship. I just told you that the rules are very strict on this planet, and I wouldn't want you getting into trouble, even though you are technically not on my crew." She paused. "At first, I thought of dropping you off on this planet, but it wouldn't be wise to drop you off on a military world. Instead we will drop you off somewhere else."

Raiden stared at her, then shrugged. "If it's the rules you're worried about, then problem solved, Captain. I can't use magic, so even if I wanted to get in trouble I can't. I'll be fine. Melinda said she'd accompany me. Would that put your mind at ease?"

Visaka looked at Melinda, who nodded. Melinda knew this planet, and if she would be accompanying him she would keep him out of trouble for sure. But why hadn't Melinda said something about it to her?

Cork came forward and handed Raiden a brand-new suit of battle armor. "And he would be wearing this armor, which would definitely help him."

"I can't use magic armor. You know that," Raiden said, frowning.

"This isn't magic armor, newbie," Cork said. "This is battle armor they used to make when we had foot soldiers, before magic was so common."

"How is this different that the previous one?" Raiden asked.

"It provides a boost to the wearer's physical strength and agility, but I didn't know they still made these," Visaka said. She was taught about this kind of armor in history classes but had never seen it with her own eyes.

"Even I thought they'd stopped making it, but I found one on the ship we raided a couple of days back, and I have a perfect pig to wear it." Cork grinned.

Raiden chuckled. "You mean guinea pig, don't you?"

Visaka found it comforting to see Cork getting friendly with Raiden. Then again, Raiden would be saying goodbye soon, so it didn't matter.

"Very well," Visaka said. "You can go if Melinda is accompanying you. But I don't want any trouble. We are already neck deep in it, and I would hate to have any more coming our way." She sighed, knowing she had a lot to achieve on that Situla IV. But first, she needed to contact Grizzy, her friend back on Titan. She would only contact him through a neutral planet to avoid any risk of him being dragged into the mess she'd started few years back.

Chapter 21

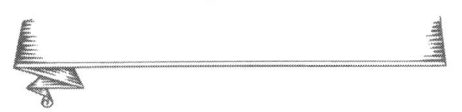

MELINDA

Melinda was almost ready when the ship docked on Situla IV. She made sure she had everything needed for trade: gold and some tradable magical artifacts. She wanted to make sure she could help Raiden as much as possible. Whenever she looked at Raiden, she remembered her brother, who was like him, a mage with very limited magic.

She remembered the tough years she spent on Titan, serving the royal family. Before becoming Visaka's personal bodyguard, she had been chief of the Royal Guard for ten years. One day, the king had asked her to act as Visaka's bodyguard, as the young princess had been a troubled child from the start. She had accepted the job, and over the years she and Visaka became friends. Their bond grew so close that she chose to leave Titan when Visaka asked.

When she had first met Visaka, the princess was just twelve years old. Visaka had tremendous magic power from childhood, a prodigy in the magical world, and she was bold enough to be proud of it. She was always a tomboy, at least until she met Richard.

Melinda's parents had wanted a boy. They had kept trying, and along with Melinda, her parents had ten girls. The year

Visaka was born, a new magical test tube fertilization method was born, which provided a chance to produce a child with immense magical power. Melinda's parents had jumped into that program, and it failed miserably. All of the children born out of that experiment lacked any potent magic. They had the least magical ability in the whole universe. Raiden still beat them, though.

When Melinda's mother first saw her son, Aaron, she displayed joy that even a one fifty year old woman may not be capable of. Melinda was overwhelmed with happiness when she saw her mother jumping up and down in the air. Her mother threw a party for the first time in her life.

Melinda's mother wished for a prosperous future for Aaron. Why wouldn't she? All of her daughters had earned high ranks in the Royal Army. Her firstborn, Melinda, was the chief of the king's guards. She envisioned a great place of power for her children. She once told Melinda that she would like to see her son go as high as a king's aide on the political ladder. A king's aide was the second highest powerful magic user on any world. The king's aide was the voice of the king when the king attended conferences on other worlds. But Aaron had limited power and couldn't even conjure a basic spell, not even after being trained by an expensive private tutor.

Aaron never excelled at anything magic-related, but he was good at painting and art. Sadly, he put it out of his mind in order to please their mother. Melinda had always wished he had tried art as a career rather than wasting years of his life trying to learn magic.

Raiden knocked on her cube's door. "Are you ready?"

Melinda looked at Raiden and was reminded of her brother. Raiden was similar to Aaron in many ways. He was trying to achieve what was impossible for him, if anyone. She doubted even someone as powerful as a king's aide could succeed at fighting dark mages in the heart of the Quantum Zone. Dark magic had always been overwhelming for human mages. It was only because of the mage emperor's powerful magic and multiple kings' combined wards that the perimeter of their world was impenetrable by dark mages. Raiden kept asking if he could get his mate back, but Melinda didn't believe he ever would. She'd help him anyway. She could at least give him a means to succeed. Even if it gave him a one percent chance, that would be better than nothing.

"A moment please," she said and picked up her staff.

"A staff?" Raiden said, looking at her. "You're like a witch out of a story."

"What is a witch?"

"Come on, don't tell me you don't know about witches." He looked surprised. "They're like mages, but only female. Anyway, what's the staff for?"

"It has two benefits. First, it advertises my rank among the mages, and second, it has a word of power inside it which doubles my magic power." Only high-level magicians could hold a staff like hers, and most of the time the presence of a staff only helped the magician accelerate their work. Magicians held great weight in society, and she was going to use that to their advantage if needed.

"Wow, I didn't know something like this existed. So, anyone can steal it from you and become powerful?"

She giggled at his naïveté. "No one else can wield it. You need to be a level five mage to hold it, and becoming a level five mage is very difficult. It requires lots of real world experience, not just academy training. Also, it was linked to my DNA when it was created for me. Every Chief of Royal Guard gets one of their own."

"Chief of Royal Guard?" Curiosity lurked in his eyes.

Now that was something she didn't want him to know about. "Nothing that concerns you."

He shrugged and walked toward the airlock. She noticed an armored collar peeking out of his shirt neck. He was wearing the armor Cork had given him. Excellent choice.

Melinda wondered what else Cork got from that ship. He had been always the sneaky one, and most of the time he irritated her. She liked people with discipline, and Cork didn't have a disciplined bone in his body. "Good. Do you feel any different, wearing that armor?"

"Not much. But I do feel lighter than normal, like gravity isn't pulling me down as much."

"Do you mind trying to jump once we are outside?" she asked.

"Sure, why not?"

※

MELINDA WAS RIGHT TO ask Raiden to jump. Once all the time-consuming customs duties were settled by the captain, they were able to get out on the street. The first thing Raiden tried was to jump, and he jumped thirty feet in the air effortlessly. His fall was less than graceful. He landed on his ass, then cursed her for asking him to jump.

Melinda stood there giggling at him while he stood and rubbed his ass.

He glared at her. "That wasn't funny at all."

"Come on, it was hilarious. Who in the world jumps so high, just to land on his own ass!" she giggled once more.

Raiden ignored her and looked around, his eyes darting from one thing to another.

"All of this must be new to you, isn't it?" Melinda asked.

"Yes, it's all so... blue," he said. "Are there any blue aliens living on this planet?"

"No aliens, only humans. Though, these worlds were inhabited by some intelligent species before we came here. All that remains of them are their temples and some buildings." She paused, "After the discovery of magic and hyperdrives, humans spread across the universe. Their advance continued until they encountered dark mages. A thousand years back, the great war of mages happened, in which the mage emperor defeated the dark general leading the war. A truce took place, and dark mages were pushed back into the Quantum Zone."

"I can't believe we humans are the only ones who live in the whole universe." Raiden looked overwhelmed by that fact.

"Well, we know only half of our galaxy. We don't know what lies in other galaxies. Once we discovered the dark mages, the mage emperor put a ward around our known worlds, so no ship or expedition can go beyond that perimeter. These worlds from the Archaic systems are the farthest worlds we can reach. Beyond these, no one can travel."

"But you said these worlds are neutral, right?" he asked.

"Correct. The Archaic worlds are not part of any Spectra system. All thirty Spectra systems come under the jurisdiction of the mage emperor." Granted, Spectra 23 and 24 were on the verge of rebellion and could slip from the mage emperor's control at any time. Then there were two Eugenio worlds, who thought of themselves as the only remaining noble worlds, though their actions never resembled anything noble. The Eugenio worlds were the ones who built most of the pirate ships and supplied many black market magical artifacts. But Raiden didn't need to know the complexity of their system, at least not yet.

"Okay. So where are we going to find the crystal you mentioned?" Raiden's tone turned serious.

"I know someone here who might be able to help us."

⨯

MELINDA STOPPED OUTSIDE the fifth shop on the black market district, Situla IV's official black market. Being a neutral world allowed the planet's council to do whatever they deemed profitable, and the black market was tremendously profitable.

"This is it," Melinda said.

Raiden looked confused. "*John's Herbs*. What does he sell? Herbs?"

"Yes, herbs, but magical ones. There are many planets that possesses aura lines, the same way humans do. But these planets are dangerous."

"Do they have fireball-shooting plants?"

Melinda giggled. "Imaginative, but no. Their plant life can develop weird mutations, attract animals to them, then poison and eat them by sucking out their life force. Though many of these plants are poisonous, they're also hallucinogens. The mage emperor banned these plants, and whenever such a plant is spotted it is destroyed by the Royal Police Force. Here, beyond the mage emperor's influence, these the plants are treated as treasure of gold, and they're easily available." Melinda paused to take a breath.

They both entered the shop. John, the owner of the shop, sat at a table, sorting a variety of plant leaves spread out in front of him. When he glanced at the new arrivals, his face turned red, and he jumped up to run toward the back door.

Melinda predicted something like this would happen, so she was ready. She waved her staff, and a fireball shot at the door, declining the owner entrance. The shop owner stopped in his tracks and turned back. Melinda loosed another fireball, which hit his face point blank when he turned. John fell, unconscious.

"Did you kill him?" Raiden ran and picked him up. He checked the man's pulse. "Thank God, he's not dead yet, but if you pull that again he might be."

"Don't worry, it's just a level two spell. It won't kill a mage like him." She moved forward and channeled a bit of her healing magic into John's body.

John coughed and opened his eyes.

"If you try to run again, I will shoot a disintegrate spell," Melinda said, giving him one warning.

"Why are you here again?" John's voice was breathy; it'd take him a couple of minutes to catch his breath. "Why are you here? I didn't do anything wrong."

"I want some information. If you don't give it to me, I will just kill you and walk away," Melinda answered coldly. Puny criminals like him didn't deserve any sympathy.

"Ask, and I shall answer what I know."

"Where can I get the dark crystal? They call it the Crystal of Quantum."

"Why do you need that? Isn't it banned by your great emperor?"

Melinda waved her staff to conjure a small fireball.

"Wait! Stop, I'll tell you about it!" He took a deep breath and looked around, like he was afraid of the words he was about to say out loud being overheard. "Zumi has that stone."

With a simple flick of her hand, the fireball hit John in the face.

"Why did you do that?" Raiden grabbed her staff. "He was answering our questions."

Melinda's stomach twinged. He was touching her staff. He wasn't supposed to be able to touch her staff. "He is lying."

"How can you be so sure?"

Melinda closed her eyes. She could see the fiery night and the battle on Titan, the powerful spell she'd unleashed and the ashes that remained in its wake. "Because I killed Zumi ten years ago."

Chapter 22

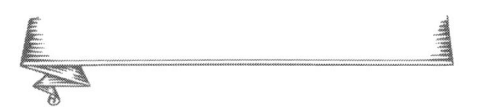

RAIDEN

"What was that?" Raiden asked, certain he couldn't have heard that right.

"I said, I killed Zumi ten years ago," Melinda said with a grimace. A fireball swirled in her hand, primed to hit the shop owner again.

Raiden stared at the red and yellow haze of the fireball in her hand. It was just an inch above her palm, but it wasn't burning her. He had seen magic being used around him for some time now, and every time he saw something new, he wished he could do it.

He grabbed Melinda's staff and pulled it down. "Let's not kill him yet. We need answers, and we have many other methods we can use." He might not be able to perform magic, but interrogation, he could do. He had learned many techniques in the military.

"We don't have time. I will make him spill the truth. Do me a favor. Look around for a plant darker than black, and get couple of leaves for me. But remember, do not touch it with your bare hands."

"No worries, I've got this kick-ass armor." He smiled at the feel of the armor. It was something special. At first, he hadn't felt anything other than a sensation of lightness, but as soon as he jumped in the air, he knew it was way more powerful than he'd thought. He could feel his agility level zooming to the sky.

He walked through the shop, finding himself surrounded by row after row of plants placed neatly on tables. Finding the darker than black plant wasn't a difficult thing. He quickly grabbed few leaves and returned to Melinda. By the time he got back, Melinda had tied the shop owner to a chair with some rope.

Melinda took the leaves from Raiden and crushed them between her gloved hands. She then put the crushed leaves in the owner's mouth and made him chew them.

"What's so special about these leaves? And why did you crush them?" Raiden asked.

"The leaves come from a plant called Kitava. It is said that it was mutated by the essence of Kitava's weapon, a dual-headed axe, just like Cork's. I don't know how much truth there is to that, but in many places this plant is used as truth serum," Melinda said.

"Finally, something I understand. Let's hope he talks." Raiden looked at the owner, who now emitted a dark aura. "What's that dark light around him?"

"That's the effect of high level magic." Melinda pulled the man's head up and slapped him with her other hand. "John, give me the honest answer. Where is the crystal?"

"Zumi has it," the owner said in a robotic voice.

Raiden assumed that, too, was an effect of the plant.

"How is it possible? She's been dead for ten years." Melinda's fingers clenched in a fist and drew back, poised to punch.

"I don't know. She lived on and established a stronghold on Situla IV. She now employs four level three mages and a bunch of marines," John said.

"That's not good," Melinda whispered.

"Why not?" Raiden asked. "How strong is she? You defeated her once, can't you do it again?" Raiden hoped the answer was yes.

"It was different then. I had access to many things. I'm low on resources right now." Melinda's tone changed a lot when she responded.

"Don't worry. You have me now. Magic or no, we'll defeat her." He didn't know how he would pull it off, but there was no way he was backing down now. Anna was waiting for him, and he would do anything to get her back, even if it required him to sacrifice his own life.

"Yes, if she is alive then I will kill her again. I can't let her live after what she has done to my sister." A tear rolled down her cheek.

Raiden felt her pain and touched her shoulder. He wanted to hug her and tell her that everything would be all right, but he couldn't do it. He wasn't sure if it was an appropriate thing in this world. Instead he just rubbed her shoulder. "Ask him her whereabouts. We can ambush her tonight."

"Where does she live these days?" Melinda asked.

"She has a palace located to the north, outside the city," John answered.

Melinda cut him loose, and they walked out.

"Will he live?" Raiden asked.

"Yes, but he won't be opening his eyes for couple of days."

"Hmm." He had suspected that there had to be some side effects to the drug. There always were.

※

IT TOOK THEM A COUPLE of hours to reach the north doors of the city via the public transport system. The city was surrounded by a huge desert on three sides, and its denizens had built large walls and placed magical wards to keep the sand away. Still, those rich enough to afford it lived in palaces outside the city. Melinda had visited the city quite a few times, so she provided him the history while they traveled to the north gate on a big cozy bus that floated five feet above the ground. Raiden suspected it ran on an anti-gravity or a magnetic field.

"Why isn't magic used for transport systems?" Raiden asked as they got off the bus at the north gate.

"There are many reasons. First, it's not a Spectra world—those have tremendous resources and gold. Second, a mage would be required to operate the bus, and mages are better paid for other things, like mining resources from the gas giants or asteroid belts. Everyone can use magic, but not everyone is a mage capable of powering up a large thing like this bus," Melinda said. "And mages don't require a bus to travel. Look outside." She pointed to his right.

A mage in gray robes was traveling through the air using fire circles. He stood on one for a moment, and when another circle of fire formed a few feet ahead, he jumped on it and the previous one vanished. He was making steps of fire to run across.

"That's amazing. Can you do that?"

"You bet I can, but I don't. When I was on Titan, I had a small pod I could charge with magic and go anywhere I wanted." She sighed.

Raiden wondered how much power Visaka had required to utilize the whole ship's systems when she connected to the magic-interfacer. He remembered she was a jumper class mage. He should ask Melinda about these classes one day. They sounded interesting. He wondered what class he would fit into. If he had any magic.

Melinda stopped after fifteen minutes of walki down a less-traveled road. "I think that's it."

Raiden looked in the direction she was looking. He found a big palace, similar to what he had seen in kid's movies. The similarities between the current time and the fiction books from his time was intriguing. "That's huge. How are we going to get in? They must have a defense system in place." There was no way the system was unguarded.

"It should be a normal access key system. The real challenge is the four mages and handful of marines that should be guarding the palace."

"Would she have some servants?" Raiden asked.

"She's bound to have some, if she owns a palace like this."

"I've got an idea. Let's get closer to the palace and scope it out," Raiden said.

They walked closer to the palace and hid behind a large rock. Raiden spotted cameras on the palace walls, and he bet they were either magical or high resolution, able to pick up anything around them. He couldn't take a chance with them.

Hours passed. Sandy wind bit their faces, but they remained hidden, watching for someone to come out of the palace. Melinda started making some low-key sounds, moving here and there, while Raiden remained silent and steady in one position.

"Aren't you bored by waiting?" Melinda asked.

"Patience is part of my training. We had to wait for days, sometimes." Raiden remembered one of his missions in Afghanistan where he had to wait in a ruined house for the target to show up. When the target changed his plans, they were stranded there for three days with minimum food.

Raiden spotted dust kicked up in the direction they had come from. "I think someone's coming." Sure enough, a small car drove up the road. By the looks of it, it could only seat a couple of people in it. "I'm going in." Raiden pushed off the ground and jumped in the air, landing on the hood of the car. The car was hovering like the bus had, so when he landed on the hood, the car lost its balance and tipped over.

A man in a black suit jumped out of the car. "Who the fuck are you?"

Raiden recognized that suit. It was similar to the Type Two spell'O'armor he had tried. So this guy was a marine with enough magic to shoot bolts. Raiden charged the marine, folding his legs and hitting the marine on his chest with his knees. The marine's back kissed the ground in less than a second. Raiden's suit packed a punch, and he had used it to his advantage.

Raiden spotted another man crawling out of the car from the corner of his eye. He was wearing a normal shirt and trousers. Before he could crawl out of the car completely, he was hit with a small fireball fired by Melinda.

"Now what?" Melinda asked, walking toward Raiden.

"We change clothes and sneak inside the palace in their car." He grabbed the car's right side and turned it upright with ease. "I'm loving this baby." He patted his own armor.

"Mark V, that is what your armor is called," Melinda said with a smile.

"Mark V. I like that name." Raiden smiled back.

Chapter 23

RAIDEN

Melinda changed into the marine's spell'O'armor, and Raiden pulled the other marine's shirt over his Mark V. Then they used the marine's access card to gain access to the palace.

"That was easy." Raiden felt good about their way in.

Outside of the palace was harsh desert, and it gave the palace a ruined look, but inside the walls Raiden's perspective changed completely. Lush blue flowers and green plants covered the whole garden.

"She must have spent piles of gold to get this garden set up," Melinda whispered. "Anyway, it won't be easy from here. So be prepared at all times. There are level three mages and, trust me, they are no joke. Engage wisely."

From his experience, Raiden knew magic wasn't a joke, and he would never take a mage lightly. Even though his physical strength was increased with the Mark V, he couldn't go toe to toe with a mage.

"Thanks. I'll be careful," he said, planning his strategy for the upcoming battle. He had the advantage of being faster than a normal human. If he could perform a surprise attack, he *might* have a chance of winning against a mage. Mages were stronger, but even they wouldn't be able to take a punch from his armor.

They headed into the heart of the palace, guessing Zumi would be living at the center.

No one stopped them until they reached a big corridor blocked by a glass door. Crazy decorations adorned the walls beginning at that point, but their access card didn't work on the glass door. It seemed the two guys they knocked out weren't important enough to have access to the inner levels.

"Now what?" Melinda asked, staring at the access card. "We can't blow it up. That would reveal our presence, and I don't want to face all the mages together."

Raiden looked for some other entrance. "We find another way in." He spotted a small duct on top of the door. It looked like an air ventilation duct. "Hang on, I'll be back." He pushed off the ground and jumped in the air. In the next moment, he was looking at the duct cover. There was no lock. He quickly grabbed the cover and dropped down to set it aside quietly. "I'll go see if I can open the door from the other side."

"Be careful, Raiden. I don't want to get you killed."

"Thanks, but don't worry. I'll be right back." He jumped again, and this time he dove into the ventilation duct. It was squeaky clean. Five minutes later he was on the other side of the glass door, waving at Melinda.

"Hey, you! Who are you? How did you get in here?" Someone yelled behind him.

Raiden opened the glass door. Their cover was already blown, and now it was time to fight, so he wanted Melinda at his side. The moment he opened the door, Melinda waved her staff to shoot a fireball. He circled to see the fireball stopped by a water missile. The two spells, equal in power, canceled each other out.

Raiden bolted toward the enemy mage. He looked young, in his late twenties. Before the caster could react, Raiden punched him in the face and sent him flying into the wall behind him. He crashed against the wall and fell unconscious.

"That was impressive." Melinda patted his shoulder.

"One mage down."

They moved forward only to find their path blocked by three more mages.

This is bad. Really bad.

Melinda waved her staff, and a flurry of fire bolts shot out of it toward the enemy mages. The mages were quick, and they quickly returned fire. One of them, a broad male, fired small fireballs to intercept Melinda's bolts. Another, a petite woman, cast a shield around her while the third, a broad and muscular woman, cast a big fireball that incinerated the fire bolts and quickly advanced toward Melinda.

Sure that Melinda could take care of herself, Raiden jumped toward the first man, who was busy shooting down Melinda's fire bolts. He wanted to attack him the same way he'd sent the water mage flying, but this one was faster. The mage cast a fireball with his other hand before Raiden could reach him.

Raiden jumped back to get out of the fireball's path. He paused for a moment to create a plan, then jumped in between the first and second caster and charged the second one. The first mage fired another fireball toward Raiden, making him jump away. But this time the fireball continued on its path toward the second mage, who had already conjured a shield to stop Melinda's fire bolts. Raiden's calculation was that her shield shouldn't be able to withstand both magic spells.

Raiden watched the firewall bounce off the second mage's shield. The fire bolts from Melinda bounced off too. His eyes scanned her shield.

Now what?

Raiden spotted a tiny crack on the head of the shield dome. He didn't waste any time and charged toward the crack. In blink of an eye, he crushed the shield with one hand and hit the woman with his other hand. One blow, and the woman was knocked down.

Raiden glanced at Melinda, who had switched back to fireballs again.

Raiden focused on the male caster and charged him. Whenever he got close, the mage shot a fireball from his second hand, making Raiden jump out of the way. If any one of those fireballs hit him, he would be badly injured. He couldn't take the chance, and both enemy mages stood their ground against Melinda.

Raiden ran toward Melinda. "Melinda, can you conjure a shield like them?"

Melinda scoffed. "Of course."

"Shield me." He needed a way to absorb a couple of fireballs so he could get in range.

"I can't conjure a moving shield around you."

"Damn! Can you knock one of them down with some higher-level spell?" He suspected Melinda was saving higher levels for Zumi, but it didn't hurt to ask.

"Not two-on-one. I don't have any multiple attack spells like battle mages." Melinda continued shooting fire bolts from her staff.

"Do it once I reach the second's body." Raiden charged toward the second mage, who lay unconscious.

As soon as he reached the second mage, he saw Melinda conjuring large fireball out of her staff and sending it toward the third mage. This fireball was different than others; it was larger, with a thick blue flame packed around a yellow core.

The first mage was free from defending himself from Melinda's barrage, and took advantage of the situation and shot a fireball at Melinda. Raiden grabbed the second one's body and jumped in between the first and Melinda, intercepting the fireball with the second one's body. The body Raiden held quickly caught fire and started burning. Raiden threw it down, feeling the heat even through his armor.

"Raiden, are you all right?" Melinda rushed to him.

"Two down," Raiden said, patting himself to make sure he wasn't on fire.

Melinda easily overpowered the last mage, knocking him out. But once it was done, she dropped to her knees with sweat dripping from her face. Raiden helped her up.

A clap of hands attracted their attention. "Good work, my old friend. But your advance stops here."

They turned to face a woman in her late fifties walking toward them. Twelve marines in black suits followed her in neat formation.

Raiden glanced at Melinda. Her face was red, and though fire burned in her eyes it quickly faded. Melinda dropped to her knees again, exhausted. Rage sapped her remaining energy, and Raiden watched victory slip out of their hands.

Chapter 24

RAIDEN

"Melinda, are you all right?" Raiden knelt and grabbed Melinda's shoulder, supporting her. His eyes darted between Zumi and her guards. Zumi was an intimidating woman. She wore a long robe made of white cloth, and both of her hands were covered in blue gloves decorated with red diamonds. The gloves emitted blue light. She must have been pouring her magic into those gloves to keep them emitting light.

Show-off.

Zumi also held a small staff. It was a foot long, a beautiful piece of metal and wood fused together and topped with a ruby at the tip. The ruby illuminated the staff with red light. Compared to Zumi's, Melinda's staff was a wooden stick. The vast difference in their weapons stuck with him, but he wasn't sure whose was more powerful.

Zumi's twelve bodyguards wore armor similar to Type Two spell'O'armor, so all twelve could probably wield magic. Thirteen versus two was an unfair number, and Raiden was going to change the odds. He just had to figure out how.

"Melinda, can you stand and engage the main enemy for few moments?" he asked.

Melinda managed to gain her feet. "What are you thinking, kid? She is as strong as a chief of the royal guards. Even ten years back, she was difficult to defeat, and looking at her staff now I can only assume she has gathered more power."

"I'm going to target the guards behind her. Thirteen against two are unfair odds, and I'm going to even them."

"Okay. Here I go." Melinda conjured a fireball even larger than he had seen before, easily one meter wide. Power rippled from the core of the fireball and radiated enough heat to make Raiden feel uncomfortable, even though he was standing couple feet away.

How much magic she is putting into that?

She could have easily destroyed all the twelve men with that fireball.

Melinda fired the ball toward the twelve men, but Zumi was quick to jump in between and nullify the spell with her own fireball, which was just as strong as Melinda's. Zumi had conjured hers quicker than Melinda. She was strong, really strong, or Melinda had become weak.

Raiden jumped in the air and landed in between them, his fist striking the ground with as much force as he could muster. The impact was so strong that the guards nearest to him were thrown back. He took advantage of the situation and knocked four of the standing ones down with a roundhouse kick. So far, none of the mages he'd faced had good physical strength. His kick combined with the power of his armor easily knocked them down.

"That's impressive, whoever you are." Zumi spoke in her delicate voice.

Four down, eight to go.

Raiden took a quick running stance and dashed toward the four guards who were trying to stand up.

His head and shoulder collided with them, knocking them back down. He stood, and with a straight kick knocked out one, then another, then another, but the fourth one had already jumped back.

Raiden faced five of them now, back on their feet and shooting various spells at him. Three fireballs and two water jets raced toward him.

A large fireball from Melinda blasted the first two guards, resulting in an explosion that set the guards on fire. The flaming guards fled, but the remaining three were quick enough to get out of the blast radius. They were not quick enough, however, to dodge Raiden's roundhouse kick. He succeeded in knocking two of them out easily.

Raiden paused, his heart beating so fast that it made him worried for a moment, but when he glanced back at Melinda he found her in worse condition. She sat on the ground, sweat running down her face. Even drained of magic, she smiled at him.

His fingers clenched in a fist. His lack of magic was hurting him and his friends now. If only he could help Melinda somehow...

He didn't have much time to think as the remaining marine cast a jet of water at him. He jumped in the air and leaped on the marine, but the marine was quick enough to avoid his kick. The marine jumped back, and again shot a water jet toward him. Raiden dodged it and charged the marine with all his might.

Raiden was a foot away from the marine when he fired a water missile from his other hand. Raiden ducked down and put all his force in an uppercut to send the marine flying toward the roof.

Raiden fell on his knees. Fatigue crawled through his body. He turned toward Zumi, who was watching him carefully. "You're next," he groaned.

"Melinda, I must say I'm impressed by your puppet here. His reflexes are quite acrobatic. But I don't get it, why is he using old battle armor? And where is his magic? If you didn't have any gold for spell'O'armor, you could have asked me for some." She giggled.

Melinda didn't take the teasing lightly. Still kneeling, she conjured and shot a spell toward Zumi.

Zumi easily nullified it with her own fire bolt, leaving a tiny puff of smoke behind.

"Do you really think I can be tricked by your level two spells? Come on, draw something above level four if you have the energy left," Zumi teased Melinda again.

Raiden watched Melinda. She wasn't holding back. The level two spell she had just cast had been a struggle. He didn't understand the levels of spells, but he got the impression that the more advanced the spell, the more magic it drained from the caster. He had seen what happened to a mage when he or she went overboard with magic. He had attended Visaka in the medical bay twice for that reason. He rushed to Melinda.

"Melinda, let's get out of here. She's powerful, and you're tapped." He would be giving up on his dream, but what use would the crystal be if he had to let his friend die for it?

Melinda pushed him away and started conjuring a cloud of fire around her staff. "No. We are settling this here and now."

Raiden watched as her body started glowing with a yellow aura. She was using a very advanced spell, and Raiden knew what the cost she would bear for casting that spell would be.

"Melinda, please, no." He tried to touch her, but he was pushed back by the energy around her.

Melinda rose into the air and twirled around, pulling the air along with her. The air around her became dense and started vibrating because of the fire magic she emitted.

Raiden jumped back to get away from her. He would have been incinerated if he had stayed there any longer.

Melinda's hands extended forward, and she channeled her blue fire beam toward Zumi. Even at four feet's distance, Raiden could feel the power of her spell.

Zami's eyes widened, but she quickly changed her stance and closed her eyes. Her body rose in the air too, and the space around her started changing its color to yellow. She was drawing a same intensity spell as Melinda, but she was holding back a little. She too channeled the fire around her staff and beamed it toward Melinda.

The two elements met at the center between the two mages, and a splash of power rippled away from the point of impact. The power of the collision was so strong that Raiden was thrown back against a wall, along with the knocked-out marines. Unfortunately, one marine had been too close to the point of impact. His body disintegrated into to ashes before Raiden's eyes.

Raiden tried to move, but moving even an inch was impossible. His plan was to hit Zumi by jumping at her, but he just couldn't push forward.

Both the ladies were giving one hundred percent with those spells. Moments passed, and Melinda's energy started to flag. Slowly but steadily, Zumi's beam pushed forward, overpowering Melinda's. In about thirty seconds, Melinda would be turned to ashes.

Raiden roared and pushed forward with all the might he had. He managed to advance a step, but lost control and was thrown back again. He dug his fingers in the floor below, and then used all his might to dash forward. His armor reacted to his need, and the next moment he was standing next to Melinda. Her eyes were closed and her body ready to give up any time. Still, she was holding her spell with sheer willpower. Zumi's beam was almost on Melinda. He knew what he had to do. Even if it killed him, he would be happy in the afterlife that he'd saved life of a friend.

Raiden shouldered Melinda aside and extended his left hand to counter Zumi's beam. He watched his Mark V's sleeve shredded to pieces wherever the fire beam touched, but his hand didn't feel a damn thing. The fire beam was vanishing into his bare hand. He glanced at Zumi, who stopped her beam and stared at him with an awestruck expression.

His body heated up, and then his right hand started shaking. He brought it forward to check what was happening. It glowed with a yellow aura. Somehow, he was holding fire magic inside his body. For the first time, for a fleeting moment, he felt what was it like to have magic inside him. Then he fell down in exhaustion, but before his eyes closed he felt a beam of fire passing out of his right hand.

Chapter 25

RAIDEN

Raiden opened his eyes to find a white ceiling overhead with lots of golden symbols embossed on it. He tried to get up, but found his ass sucked into an inch-thick soft bed. The bed was surrounded by thick white curtains, which bore the same golden symbols on the ceiling.

Am I dead?

It didn't look like heaven or hell, though. He rose from the bed, pushing the curtains aside. The room was filled with unfamiliar décor. There was a single window. Raiden looked outside, finding a garden with green and blue grass covering the ground. He remembered seeing that garden before.

"I wondered when you would wake up." Zumi's delicate voice made him turn back.

She stood at the door with the same smug smile she'd worn when they first met, but the left side of her body was wrapped in a bandage. A similar bandage covered Raiden's right arm.

"What's going on? What happened to you? " He was missing something. "Wait... Where's Melinda? Did you kill her? I swear to God, if she's dead, I'll kill you with my bare hands." He bolted toward her.

"Calm down, warrior. She is safe and under observation in the next room." Zumi waved her hand and a display appeared out of thin air. It showed Melinda lying on a bed similar to his own.

"Why's she sleeping?"

"She was exhausted by that level five spell. She will wake up in a day or two. I'm surprised you are awake already, so soon after consuming my level five spell." She walked closer, lifting his hand and looking it over with admiration.

"What really happened? How did I survive?" If he had been hit by level five spell, he had to be dead. Who injured Zumi? Did Visaka and the others attack her? That didn't make sense, either. How would be Zumi alive if they had?

"Don't you remember? The energy beam you sent at me?" She stared at him. "Come on, it took me by surprise. And this happened." She looked at her bandage.

"The beam? What beam? I don't know what you mean."

"Come on. You fired a disintegrate spell, and you don't even remember it?"

"I don't have any magic inside me."

"No, that's not true. You have magic, plenty of it. You have a special kind of magic, dark magic, something that can only be wielded by a dark mage from the Quantum Zone. I don't know what sorcery Melinda did with you, but you are the rarest species I have ever seen in this universe. A human mage with dark magic. I can't believe this is even possible." She paused to study him further. "Now tell me why are you here? Did you come here to kill me? Or did the Chief of Guard bind you to do her dirty work?"

"Don't be ridiculous. Melinda didn't do anything to me. We're here for a crystal that will let me travel through the fourth dimension." Raiden paused to consider if he should be revealing his true motives. What the heck, if she'd wanted to kill him she would have done it already. "I want to use it to save my love, Anna, who was captured by the dark mages." He told Zumi his story from the beginning.

She listened to him with an amused smirk.

"You're saying you were initiated by a dark mage? That's unheard of. Wait, let me see your hand." She pulled the bandage off his hand, revealing a thick, black ring around his wrist.

"What's this? What did you do to my hand?" Raiden tried to rub the ring off, but it didn't vanish. The dark circle was a permanent stain on his wrist now.

"Can you take couple of steps backward?" Zumi asked.

He groaned. "First tell me what the fuck this thing is."

"Let's test if my theory is correct."

He followed her instructions.

"I will fire a basic spell, which shouldn't hurt you. Use your left hand to absorb it," she said.

"What? I can't do that. I can't absorb magic." But wait. He had done that, hadn't he?

"Let's test this, warrior." Without saying anything further, she shot a small fireball at him.

Raiden instinctively put his left hand up, and the fireball was absorbed by his hand. He stared at his hand, which pulsed with fire magic. His right hand started shaking. He knew what was happening now, so he directed his right hand toward the wall in front of him. A large fireball emerged out of his right hand and shot forward. The fireball created a large hole in the wall and passed through it.

He stared at his hands in disbelief. "What's happening to me?" Something was wrong with him, and he didn't understand it at all.

Zumi giggled. "Fascinating. You are a dark mage after all."

Chapter 26

VISAKA

Visaka walked through the lanes of Situla IV, searching for Trisha's Tech Shop, which reportedly had the best deals on starship parts at the Situla IV black market. She wondered about the name, but her source guaranteed that it was the best in town. After searching through five lanes of the black market, she found the shop. It was a small shop with a scant ten by ten square feet of carpet space.

She entered the shop, searching for some clue to prove it was the right one. She was told that this shop sells spaceship modules, but looking at it, she felt it sold squat. The shop had just one large counter. A lady wearing big spectacles sat behind it, reading a book.

"How can I help you, miss?" The lady adjusted her specs.

"Is this Trisha's Tech Shop?" Visaka asked.

"Yes, and you are talking to her."

Visaka's wary eyes surveyed the shop, again trying to find something to convince herself that she was in the right place.

"We deal in starship tech parts. If you're wondering why the shop is so small, rest assured. We have a warehouse right beside the starport, and whatever you buy will be delivered within forty-eight hours." She gasped for breath. "Now again, how can I help you ma'am?"

"Oh, yes, I'm so sorry," Visaka said.

"I understand, I get that asked a lot. So, what are you looking for? A spellcannon? Or a spell-laser? We have those too, but they're expensive for what they do. You would be better off with the spellcannon, if you ask me. Old school, but effective."

Visaka shook her head to say no, but the lady continued talking.

"I think you need the Type Six spell'O'armor, don't you? It's the latest on the market, capable of holding out against ten level three mages. It's just awesome. Your marines would love it." Trisha got a bit dreamy-eyed.

"I'm looking for an extra cylinder module for starship T100."

Trisha blinked, snapping out of her daydream. "T100? That's a damn old ship. I've got a T950 for sale. It was in service till last year, and I'll make you a great deal."

"Sorry, but I need this specific module only." Visaka prayed she'd find at least one of the modules she required. Her ship was very old and had been out of production for almost seven hundred years. With the money she had when she left Titan, it was all she could afford. She'd found it on sale from a black-market dealer, and got it for just five hundred million gold. Considering her tight finances, she'd had to take it. Even hundred year old models started at two thousand million gold chips, which would have emptied almost half of her cache.

"We don't have one right now, but I can procure it for you." Trisha looked disappointed.

"Wow, does someone still make them?" Visaka couldn't help but ask.

"Not, but I know of a stash of broken-down T100's on a distant planet, and I'm sure we can find an oxygen module from one of them. There are no mechanical or magical parts in them, so they should be safe unless there is some leakage."

"That's great, how much would it cost?" Visaka held her breath.

"Fifty million gold. Normally they would go cheap for new ships, but I need to get this from another planet so there are transportation costs added to the bill."

"I'll take it." Visaka relaxed with a sigh. Fifty million was still a lot, but it was better than not having a module at all. That one module would add one week of range to her ship.

"Half the payment must be made in advance."

"Sure." Visaka pulled up her electronic chip for payment.

Trisha got out her payment receiver. Visaka was about to put her chip in when two mages entered the shop.

"Hey, babe, is this Trisha's shop?" one of them asked.

"Yes, how can I help you, sir?" Trisha discreetly traded the payment receiver for a small staff tucked under her desk.

Visaka stepped aside. The Trisha girl was surely a high-class mage. Only level five mages could wield a weapon like a staff and use it at their will. If she was worried about these guys, then Visaka should worry about them, too.

"We want to buy a simulation module for our K500 ship. Do you know the latest one that makes you feel wonderful?" One of them winked at Trisha.

Visaka had heard about these modules. They were nothing but banned simulation modules that ran a sex simulation for the users. Well, not banned in this side of the universe, actually.

"We don't deal in those modules. You can try another shop," Trisha replied calmly, but her tone had changed, becoming colder.

"That's a bummer," one of the mages said. " Aman, let's try the next shop. This one was supposed to be the best on this planet, but I guess not."

"Yerra, did you hear about the coup on Spectra 33?" Aman commented to his companion while they walked out of the shop.

They grabbed Visaka's attention as soon as they spoke the word Spectra 33. It was her home world.

"Trisha, can I come back later? I guess I forgot my other payment chip on the ship." She glanced back at the shop owner.

"Yes, of course. We are open all days." Trisha was back to her normal self.

Visaka left the shop and began following the mages at a distance. She waved her right hand to cast a simple level one air spell that made the words from their mouths flow on a stream of air to her ears. It was a handy spell. Visaka had learned it from a particular spy. She sighed at the memory of that spy. It was part of her past, her bloody, painful past.

"Yerra, that chick behind the counter was super cute, wasn't she?" Aman said.

"I liked the other one. If we could just get them alone..." He chuckled.

Visaka shivered at the objectification, but men would be men.

The two mages continued talking about things which Visaka had no interest in. She wanted to know about her home planet. They walked toward a big building located at the end of the lane. Once they went inside, her spell would stop working.

She had to make a decision now, whether to let them walk into the building and forget about the information they carried or catch them before they left and get the information from them. She thought for a moment, but couldn't make up her mind because she didn't know what their power levels were. It was quite the dilemma, but she decided to take action.

"Gentlemen," she called.

They both turned and smiled at her.

"You are the lady from the shop. Good, the Lord must be pleased with us today." Aman smiled at her, but there was animosity in his eyes.

"You were talking about the coup on Spectra 33. I want to know more about it."

Their stance changed. One of them pulled a spellpistol out of his pocket, and the other one waved his hands to conjure a fireball.

"So, you won't give information without a fight, huh?" Visaka said and drew her magic out on her palms.

Chapter 27

VISAKA

Visaka's eyes were fixed on the spellpistol wielder, Aman.

How did he get it through security? Spellpistols were high-class weapons built like staffs, bound to a caster by a word of power. With the help of technology, spellpistols could do many things a staff could never do, like morphing the spell into pure energy bullets that packed a strong punch in a tiny magic bullet. A staff could never do that. She would never want to be at the receiving end of a magic bullet.

"Why do you want it?" Aman asked.

"It doesn't concern you. I'm asking nicely and expect a reply without having to use force." The air around her took the shape of a thick air ball. It looked small, but a knowledgeable user would recognize it as a level four spell, capable of taking down dozens of mages with one swipe.

"Yerra, that's a level four mage, so don't try anything stupid," Aman told his friend.

But the other guy seemed to be a hothead. Before his friend could finish his sentence, he had shot his fireball toward her.

Visaka flicked her other hand and deflected the fireball. Level two spells didn't have any effect on her. Even if that fireball had hit her, she would have walked away unscathed thanks to her superior physical endurance.

Aman groaned. "I told you not to do anything supid!" He faced Visaka. "Lady, I don't know who you are, but we don't want any trouble here. So, I suggest you walk out, and we will do the same."

"I can't." She wouldn't go back to her ship without the information. She had to know what they knew about her planet, even if it meant risking her stay on this planet by breaking the law against magic use.

"Why are you being nice to this bitch? Just fire your Goddamn pistol already!" Yerra threw another fireball at her.

This time Visaka ducked and dodged it. It was too slow to catch her unaware. In her left hand, she conjured a level two air bolt and fired it at the fire magic user.

Aman jumped in front of Yerra and deflected the spell with his free hand. "Are you crazy, Yerra? Did you even notice she has a level four air ball in her right hand, and she has been maintaining it for the last three minutes? She is clearly out of your league." He faced Visaka, "Miss or missus, I would suggest you walk away from here. Attack again, and I won't hesitate to fire this." He gestured with his pistol.

Visaka studied his pistol. It could be deadly for her if this Aman guy was a level four or beyond mage.

She poured more magic into the level four spell she was holding and shrunk it further. Her body began emitting a blue aura.

"Yerra, get out of here," Aman said, in a serious tone. He pushed his friend behind him and fired an electric bolt from his pistol.

Visaka jumped in the air and dodged the electric bolt. "So, you are a lightning mage. A rare type of magic. I bet that makes you a highly sought mage."

She shot the level four spell she was saving toward Aman, who countered it with a level four ball lightning blast. Their spells collided in midair, and the impact rippled through the air around them. Visaka and Aman used magic to maintain their position, but Yerra was thrown against a nearby wall.

This is bad. Aman was a level four mage, and he could conjure level five spells with the help of his pistol. She studied them both. Aman looked confident enough, but Yerra looked frightened by the display of their powers.

Visaka charged Yerra, but before she could get to him Aman fired another electric bolt at her. She countered, and when their spells canceled each other out, the walls next to the impact point disintegrated.

Visaka's energy began to wane. She had to be careful now. She didn't have enormous reserves of energy to cast multiple level four spells. In a good day she could cast only ten or fifteen of such bolts. If she had access to her staff, she could have cast maybe twenty. The pistol user was at an advantage here; he could easily cast fifty level four spells with level three spell energy, thanks to his pistol. If they continued, he would overpower her in no time.

Visaka closed the distance between her and Yerra. Aman fired another level four bolt, which she nullified using an air shield. Her precious necklace stored some power of her for such times, and she needed only a few moments of uninterrupted time to capture the fire mage.

She wrapped her arm around his neck and conjured a level three spell in her free hand, directing it at his heart.

Aman looked frustrated. "Come on dude, I clearly told you to run away."

"Please, bro, save me from this chick. She will kill me if you don't tell her what she wants to know." Yerra began to cry.

"Disgusting soldier, you can't cry in front of the enemy," she criticized.

"She is right, man. You can't cry when you get captured by the enemy." Aman holstered his pistol. "Okay, miss, ask what you want to know. But first promise me that you won't kill my brother."

"Brothers?" She glanced between them in confusion. Yerra was a large black man, while Aman was a small white one. How could they be brothers?

"We are magic brothers, bound by magic, not by blood," Yerra rumbled.

"Whatever, I don't like to get my hands dirty for no apparent reason," Visaka said.

"Okay, then ask away," Aman said.

"Tell me everything you know about this Spectra 33 coup."

"Well... okay, here it goes. Legion worlds, are you aware of them?" he asked.

"Yes." She sighed. A close someone had served as a spy on those worlds for years, and she knew all that was happening there.

"Then you must be someone who has access to the important people of Spectra 33. Tell me what you know, and I can fill in the rest," Aman said.

She thought about it. It'd been years since she left Titan, but she always kept tabs on the information that flowed in pirate channels, especially anything about her world.

"I've heard about the revolt on Ambala, but nothing after that." She had heard stories of the Royal Navy and army destroying cities to overcome that revolt. It was something she never liked, but a king's resolve to keep his citizens safe was greater than the puny wishes of her or anyone like her.

"That was a coup planned by the prince of Spectra 33 against the king."

"How is that even possible? The prince has been dead for long time!" she screamed in anger. The air spell she held moved a bit closer to Yerra, cutting a bit into his skin like a blade. "Don't give me shit, man. I will kill this man if you lie again."

"I'm afraid that my information is most accurate. I saw the prince taking part in the battle of Ambala." Aman's tone was steady.

"It's not possible, because I killed him with my own hands." A tear dropped down her face. She was the princess who killed her own brother and then ran away in fear for her life.

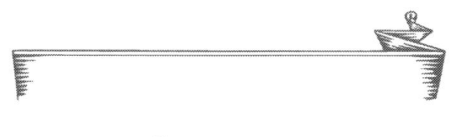

Chapter 28

VISAKA

Aman chuckled. "Wow, you are really her. The infamous Princess Visaka. I knew it when I saw you in that shop. Yerra, didn't I tell you she was the one we were looking for?"

"Yes, she is the one." Yerra smiled back and slipped away from her grip.

Visaka tried to grab him again, but either he was faster than before or she was slower than before.

"What is happening?" she asked, finding it hard to move away from where she stood.

"I might have slowed down your movements for a while. I want you to stand still while I grab your necklace," Yerra said.

"What are you talking about? Who are you guys?" Visaka asked, while trying hard to move through the barrier Yerra had placed around her. It was a level five barrier, created by a fire element user. She knew of this spell, but she hadn't thought that Yerra could cast it. How could she be so easily snared in such a foolish trap? Now that she thought about it, Yerra must have needed at least couple of minutes to conjure that spell, and she'd willingly given him that time.

"Damn you, Yerra!" She yelled in frustration, but she couldn't do anything.

"Calm down, Princess. We are just two petty thieves who collect valuable items like your necklace." Yerra moved around her and in the blink of an eye the necklace was gone from her neck.

"Please give me that back. It's the last memory I have of my mother." Tears rolled down her cheeks. How could she lose that? First, she was framed for a crime she didn't commit, then she lost her love, and then she was charged with treason against the king. Now she was stripped of the last memory of her mother, too.

"Come on, it's just a necklace. I'm sure you must have plenty of them in your stash," Aman said.

She controlled her tears. "Now what? Are you going to turn me in for the bounty set by my father?" She had faced many bounty hunters in the last three years, all after the money set by her kingly father for her head. It was ironic, but it was a frequent practice among the mage governments to declare a bounty and let pirates or bounty hunters do their job.

"No, we are not after you. And the things I have told you are all one hundred percent accurate," Aman said.

"Do you really think I would believe a thief's words? I killed my brother myself, and you are telling me that my brother is alive? Are you kidding me?" They must have thought her a fool, but she wasn't one.

"If you don't believe us, maybe you can believe this footage we have from someone who was there." Aman slipped a small data drive into her hand. "The barrier spell will vanish in five minutes. Don't even think about coming after us. You won't find us by any means." Aman waved his hands and a black hole opened. He vanished through that hole.

Fear gripped her heart. "Who are you guys?" The portal Aman had opened led to the fourth dimension, and no living human mage could do that.

"We?" Yerra turned back to face her. "We are petty thieves." He smiled at her and opened another black hole and vanished.

Visaka knew she wouldn't be able to trace either of them. No living mage could.

Five minutes passed, and the barrier around her vanished. She glanced at the data drive in her hand, then rushed toward her ship.

Chapter 29

MELINDA

Melinda woke from what felt like a long dream. Raiden sat near her head, covering his face in his hands. Black armor covered his left arm.

"Where am I?" she asked, looking around. Her ship's medical bot rushed to greet her. She was on her ship, but how was that even possible? The last thing she remembered, Zumi was overpowering her.

I must be dead. Is this the afterlife? If so, what's the medical bot doing here?

Raiden was so deep in thought, he didn't hear her.

"Raiden—" Her voice stuck in her throat. She was too weak to talk.

He jumped, almost falling from the stool he sat on, then looked at her with a wide grin. "You're awake! Relax, we're safe and back on *Challenger*."

"What happened? How are we not dead?"

"We defeated Zumi and raided the dark crystal. I haven't told anyone about it yet, and I hope you won't either."

She nodded. "How did you manage it?" There was no way Raiden could have defeated Zumi.

"Your last spell, that fire beam or whatever, it overpowered her before you collapsed. It was easy for me to finish the job after that."

"Did you kill her?" Her fingers clenched in excitement. Good news was expected.

"No, she ran away before I could. I just searched the palace and found the crystal we were looking for. And then I bought you here."

"You should have killed her when you had the chance." Her blood ran cold. She wanted Zumi dead. She had killed her before, but somehow she'd survived.

"I'm sorry, Melinda, but my priority was your safety. Plus, her magic seemed like a lot for someone like me to handle."

"I understand." He was right. He was a mere human. How could he deal the last blow, when his team mate was in danger? "What happened to your left arm?"

"Oh, this? My old armor got burned. I picked this up from a fallen mage. It looks cool even with just a hand piece, doesn't it?"

She smiled at his weird taste in armor. She couldn't understand how in the God's way he could wear a piece of hand armor that looked totally out of place and think it looked cool.

Melinda was about to say something when she heard footsteps.

Visaka came running and hugged her tightly. "Thank God, you are awake. I've got so much to talk with you about."

"I'll leave you two, then." Raiden stood and walked out.

"That kid and his weird taste in armor..." Melinda smiled, watching him go.

"I heard you faced Zumi out there. How are you holding up?" Visaka rubbed Melinda's shoulder.

"Not bad. Apparently I won the fight, but I still couldn't kill that bitch." Melinda glowered. Even thinking about Zumi made her agitated. "Anyway, how did your purchase go?" Melinda knew what Visaka was looking for, and though she disapproved of Visaka spending her personal gold, she knew how important the oxygen module was for their ship.

"Fine, but I have something to show you." Visaka turned serious. She plugged a data drive into a display near her. "It was shot six months back on Ambala."

"You mean when the revolt took place?" Melinda asked. They had heard about the revolt on a pirate communication channel.

"Yes. Watch this." Visaka turned the footage on. The camera followed a standard battle sequence, where some royal mages were fighting against rebellion mages. Visaka zoomed in on a particular frame, where it looked like the rebellion command mage was giving orders.

"What's so special about this?" Melinda asked.

"Look at him." Visaka froze the footage and zoomed in on the command mage's face. Melinda focused on the face. It was familiar, but it took a moment for it to register. "Is that Prince Victor?" She covered her mouth with her palm. "Oh God, what sorcery is this?"

"It's not sorcery, Melinda. It's a bloody setup. I need to show this to our King."

"How? We will be killed before we're even given chance to speak with anyone on Titan." If they tried to go near any of the Spectra 33 home planets, the auto-bots guarding the system would shoot them down. For criminals like them, there had been a shoot first, ask questions later policy for ages.

"I've arranged a meeting with someone on Alshat."

"Is that someone Richard?" Melinda couldn't believe Visaka. Richard was her lover and a spy on the Legion world. Those barbarians hated anyone from the Spectra royal family. How was she planning to visit that planet without getting killed?

Chapter 30

RAIDEN

Raiden tapped a button on the armored glove he wore. It was part of an ancient armor suit that Zumi had given him. He studied the black ring around his wrist and remembered the conversation they had.

"You are turning into a black mage. The more you use the magic residing in you, the more your body will be consumed by dark magic. One fine day, you'll turn into one of the hideous creatures the dark mages are."

"No, I don't believe you. I don't have magic. Melinda couldn't detect aura lines in my body." For the first time, Raiden hated the possibility of having magic.

"Because she didn't use a dark magic meter. She was checking your human aura lines. Those are two different things."

"No, she did check to see if I was a dark mage. I remember that."

"It's a bit weird, but she must have had a glitch in her meter, so you passed undetected. I have something that will decelerate this process. Or, at least I hope so. I would suggest using your powers wisely after this moment."

"How do I do that? I don't know what powers I have, much less how to use them."

"Don't forget, you absorbed a level five disintegrate spell, and then this black ring appeared around your wrist. That's your power." She paused, then added, "Wait, I will get the armor piece I have. I didn't use it, purposefully."

"What is it?"

"A magic suppressor. It's a piece of armor—who knows who made them in the first place, but if you wear it, your magic will be suppressed. It'll allow you to pass on any spell you absorb without amplifying it with dark magic."

"Fine by me." Raiden said. He knew these people didn't like dark mages, and he wasn't ready to become a creature like the ones he had seen when he first woke up. "One more thing. Is there any way to get rid of these powers?"

"I don't know. I'm only helping you because I owe that woman." She looked at the display screen, which showed Melinda, still exhausted and asleep. "I hurt her badly, once, and I still regret that."

"How do you know each other?" Raiden asked.

"We were best friends and went to the same magic academy when we were kids," she sighed. "Let me fetch you that armor."

Zumi came back with a piece of armor, just a hand piece. It looked ancient. She handed it to him, and he put it on.

"This is a piece of immortal dragon armor. Let's try this." Zumi stood next to him with a small fireball swirling in her palm.

"Are you sure it won't hurt me?"

"Come on, when did level one spells start hurting people? These are only used for igniting firewood in the kitchen."

"You guys use fire in the kitchen?" Raiden couldn't believe it. All the technological advancements he'd seen, and they were still using fire in the kitchen.

Zumi slapped her palm to her forehead. "It was just a metaphor, you duffer. Now eat this." She flung the fireball at him.

Raiden absorbed with his armored left hand. The magic swirled through his body. This time, he felt it pass through his heart and down his right arm. He could feel the magic wanting to come out, so he let it pass out of his right hand. An exact replica of Zumi's fireball came out of his right hand.

"Good, so your dark magic is not amplifying the magic anymore. It's a good start. But remember, don't use it in front of others. No one in the universe can absorb magic and fire it back like you. It's not possible with normal human magic, so you will have to lay low, or you will get caught," Zumi said.

"Yes, I understand."

Raiden returned back to the *Challenger* with Melinda, and now he studied the dark circle around his wrist.

What's happening to me? I didn't want this magic, but somehow, I'm messing everything up. How am I going to find Anna now? He had many questions, but no answers.

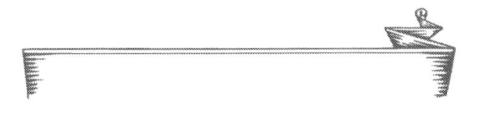

Chapter 31

VISAKA

"It was hard to contact Richard, but someone helped me get through to him," Visaka said. She knew it would be breathtakingly hard to speak with him again, but she had no other choice. It had been three years, and she was finally escaping from the pain of their breakup, but she might get pulled into her old memories again.

"Are you sure it's a good idea?" Melinda asked, her eyes still fixed on Visaka.

"No, it's not, and I know it's going to hurt. But who else I can trust with this information?" It was already breaking her heart, but after hours of thinking, she had arrived at this decision. It could have been so much better, if not for that incident where she became a villain of a whole planetary system. Regardless, she had bitten the bullet and contacted him last night. Surprisingly, he'd agreed to meet her on Alshat. Now the only question was how to reach that planet. "I'm not sure how we are going to reach Alshat in ten days, though. Richard said he has to get off-world after that, and the meeting would be very difficult once that happens."

"Just ten days? Impossible, even if we had the latest starship. And how are we going to fill our oxygen supply on the way?"

"Well, I have given it some thought, and we have another way to get there. We have the dark rune on our ship."

"No. Not again. Please. It's suicide for you. You won't be able to get up for five days after using that."

"It fits our timeline perfectly. We can jump through the fourth dimension tonight, and then I will be up and about in five days. We will save time, and Richard told me that no harm will come our way on Alshat as their generals already know about my crime. They might even reward us for killing a Spectra prince." Visaka giggled. She had learned to turn her sorrow into a joke.

"No, Visaka. We can't do that. What if something goes wrong?"

"Nothing will go wrong. Trust me. We will be all right, and once we get there we will show this message to Richard, and he will arrange everything afterward. He is very close to my father. It will be easy once he is convinced." Visaka had everything figured out. At least she thought so. Once the King knew the truth, she would be called back, and then she could see what her brother was really up to. But for starters, she was happy for the first time that her bastard brother was alive. Now she could kill him for real.

"What about you and Richard? Things turned ugly when you left Titan." Melinda held her shoulder tightly.

"I don't know, I will face it when we actually meet. But don't worry, I won't break this time. It's strictly business now." She hoped that would be the case, and she meant what she said.

She just couldn't let her emotions run wild like they did last time. The breakup with Richard had cost her emotionally, a lot, and she couldn't go through it again and again.

She still remembered that rainy night...

Chapter 32

VISAKA ...THAT RAINY night

Melinda rushed into Visaka's room like she was in a life-threatening situation. Well, she was in a grave situation, after all.

"What is it?" Visaka asked. "Please tell me something good. You know they are accusing me of a crime I didn't commit."

"The footage doesn't lie." Melinda grabbed her shoulder. "But my heart says you are telling the truth, and that's why I'm here."

"What are their thoughts?" The council was meeting today to discuss her case.

Thank God, Melinda is part of the council.

"I'm sorry, but they are going to execute you in couple of weeks. This Friday they will make the official announcement."

"No, this can't be true." She dropped on her knees. "I can't die. This is not fair. I didn't kill him! There is no way a level two spell could kill a powerful mage like him. Victor is a level five mage, why don't they understand that?" She beat her fists against the ground again and again, but nothing was going to change the council's decision. Her fate had been sealed the moment she fired that spell at her brother. If the council had decided, she would be executed on the date they chose. It was the rule of her world. The council held more power than her father, the King.

"Didn't he protest?" She searched Melinda's eyes for an answer. "No, why would he? He never thought I was anything more than an errand girl living in his palace. Death it is, then." She stood up with pride pulsing through her body. If she was going to die, why not with the pride of a mage?

"No, you're not dying. We are flying out of here." Melinda's eyes burned with a determination Visaka had never seen before.

"Flying? What do you mean?"

"I've procured a small craft for us, enough to take us to an Archaic world. We will lay low for some time and then decide what to do."

"That's a crazy thought."

"But sane enough to save your life. It's time, Visaka. A new life awaits you."

"The life of a traitor? We both will be called traitors, and bounties will be placed on our heads."

"Who cares? Pack your stuff, and we will leave the planet in few hours."

Visaka thought about it. Her mind said not to try anything stupid and to simply accept death, but her heart said to run. There might be a way to prove her innocence, after all.

"I've a little thing to take care before that," Visaka said. She knew who else would help her in this. She just needed to find him.

SHE SNEAKED INTO HIS room and hugged him tightly. "Richard."

"How are you holding up, my love?" Richard's fingers slipped through her hair and rubbed the bottom of her temple.

She soaked in the all comfort she could get from his embrace. It'd been days since she'd hugged him like this.

"They are going to execute me." Visaka burst into tears. She had managed not to break down in front of Melinda, but when she hugged Richard she just let go. He understood her better than anyone, and there was nothing she would hide from him.

"This is bad." He held her at arm's length and looked into her eyes. "What are you going to do, Visaka?"

"What do you suggest? Shall we run away? We can live on a neutral planet. Heck, we can even go to an Eugenio world and live our life peacefully." If she was going to run away, why not with Richard? He was her love, and leaving him wasn't an option. If he used his connections, she wouldn't need to take Melinda with her and could save Melinda's name in the process.

He turned away and walked to the window. Rain poured down outside, and in a flash of lightning she saw his face clearer than ever. He wasn't happy with her suggestion.

"I can't do that, Visaka. It's not a good thing for my career or my life. I've so much to achieve. I may even become a king one day. But not if I run with you tonight."

Her heart shattered to pieces.

No, he must be kidding. He would hug me anytime and say I was joking and let's get off this world.

"Don't joke, sweetie. I've time till Friday, and I know you will make the preparations."

"Believe me. I'm not going to do anything like that. And I trust that you will accept your sentence with a smile on your face. There is no better punishment than execution for a traitor."

She walked to him and grabbed his shirt and shook him. "Look in my eyes, Richard, and say that again." She paused to gauge his reaction. "We vowed to marry each other, you damn fool. Don't you love me anymore?"

"I do, but a capital punishment? Sorry, I can't do what you are asking."

The truth was in front of her eyes. He wasn't going to help her. Fleeing was something else, but betrayal from Richard? That was beyond any pain she had suffered till then.

VISAKA WAS PULLED BACK to the present by Bradok's voice on the comms.

"Captain, we have an emergency. A Royal Navy ship is showing up on the starport's radar."

"What? What are they doing here? It's unlikely that any Royal Navy ship would dock on this world. Anyway, prepare for takeoff. We have everything set up," Visaka said.

"I don't think we can. Raiden and Cork are not on board," Bradok said.

Visaka slapped her hand on the control panel next to her. She was either going to lose her friends or her life.

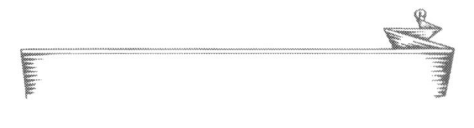

Chapter 33

RAIDEN

"What is it we're looking for?" Raiden asked.

Cork stopped humming long enough to answer. "We're buying something for the captain. A magical artifact. There is a shop in the black market that sells them."

"What magical artifact?" Raiden asked curiously.

"It is something called a mystic's crystal. And, before you ask, I don't know what it does," Cork said, smirking.

"Okay."

Cork cheered as they stopped outside a shop. "Here it is." The sign out front read "Aniket's Mystic Shop."

"That's a pretty weird name for an artifact shop," Raiden said.

"Who cares?" Cork shrugged, and they went inside.

A girl in a black robe stood behind the counter. "Good evening, gentlemen. I'm Ishita. How may I assist you?" Her dark blue eyes instantly caught Raiden's attention. There was something unusual about them.

"We are looking for a mystic's crystal. I was told you would have one," Cork said.

"Yes, we have a few, sir. Let me fetch one for you." She vanished through a door behind her.

Raiden looked over the things placed below a glass counter. There was some weird stuff there, like bones, necklaces, a few weapons, and lots of crystals.

"What kind of shop is this again?" Raiden asked.

"I guess it is something to deal with fucking strong ancient magic. It's so different from our elemental magic. I saw it used once, and it was so fucking crazy. It wiped out lots of mages in one swipe before the king could neutralize it with his wards."

Raiden moved to the second counter and found a piece of hand armor. The same as his.

Can it be a second piece of immortal dragon armor? I wonder what it does.

He couldn't stop himself and slipped his right hand under the counter and picked it up. An alarm went off.

"You pighead, what did you do?" Cork yelled, forming a lightning bolt on his hand.

"Nothing, I was just checking something out." He placed the armor on his right hand. It fit perfectly. "We'll just pay for it," Raiden said.

Ishita practically flew back through the door. "What have you done, you moron? That is a cursed piece. Why did you pick it up?" An orb of lightning hovered over one of her hands.

"Look I have another, and it doesn't curse me at all." Raiden showed her his left arm.

"Give it back, you fool, and put your tail in your ass and get out of here right now!" The girl meant business. Her lightning orb was slowly moving around her palm, gathering more energy.

"Hey how are you doing that? It's a level three spell isn't it? But how did you get it to go level four? That's not possible." Cork's voice became heavy. "Will you marry me, girl?"

"What?" Raiden and Ishita spoke at the same time, staring at Cork.

"Ignore him Ishita," Raiden said. "How much does it cost? I'm happy to pay for it. No skirmish is required."

"It's not for sale." She shot the lightning orb toward Raiden.

Raiden jumped back, but the lightning orb followed him. He flung up his right hand, curious what the new armor piece might do, and put his palm against the lightning orb, trying to absorb its magic. The orb was sucked into his body, but pain lanced his hand and spread across his body. He went numb in a second and fell on the ground, electrocuted.

"I told you it's cursed. It doesn't let you fire your magic, and sucks everything in." Ishita moved toward him slowly.

Cork jumped to his side. "Why did you do that, pighead?" He lifted Raiden in his arms and teleported them outside of the shop. "We need to get off this planet now. The black head must have called the police force already." He cursed Raiden some more and teleported again.

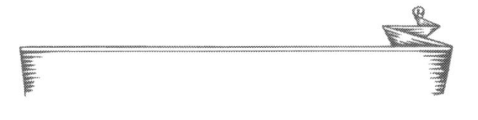

Chapter 34

RAIDEN

Raiden recovered by the time they reached their ship, but his mind was still working through what had happened at the shop. Why had the armor reacted differently to him?

The moment they entered the ship, they knew something was wrong.

"What's happening?" Raiden asked, walking onto the control bridge.

"A Royal Navy battalion is entering the planet's starport." Bradok watched a display, where five red dots slowly approached the docks.

"What the hell? What are we going to do now?" They were in big trouble. They were pirates, or at least Visaka and her team was, and pirates had plenty of reasons to hide from the Royal Navy. "There should be other pirate ships here, on account of the black market and all. Do we still have to worry about the navy? What's the chance they're here for us?"

"It's not like that, buddy. We have active bounties on our names. That's worse than being a pirate."

"What kind of bounty? Did you guys kill someone, or raid someone from the Royal Navy?" Raiden couldn't believe they were under bounties.

What kind of mess am I really in?

"I shouldn't tell you, but... why not? If you die today, you might as well die knowing the truth." Bradok chuckled.

"Come on, spill it already." Raiden's heart pumped faster. What truth was Bradok going to reveal?

"Visaka, our Captain, is wanted for killing a prince of the Spectra system."

"What the hell?" Raiden stared at Bradok in shock. It took him a moment to recover. "Did you really say she killed a freaking prince? Why would she do that?" Visaka seemed nice enough. Why go killing a prince?

Visaka rushed in and took the pilot seat. "None of your business. Bradok, why are we still here? Prepare to jump." She gave one order after another order; she was the captain, after all.

"We can't jump into hyperspace while the navy is docking. We don't have permission, Captain." Bradok was losing his patience, too.

"We are not jumping through hyperspace. I'm opening a portal to the fourth dimension," Visaka said.

Bradok's face bore a big "What the Fuck?" question mark, but he remained silent and nodded.

Visaka gave him a stern look. "It's better than dying here."

Bradok nodded again and tapped a few buttons on the control panel next to him.

The last time they'd jumped through the fourth-dimension, Raiden hadn't known squat about it. This time, he had some idea what would happen.

Visaka attached herself to the magic-interfacer.

Raiden watched them argue, but he didn't understand what the fourth dimension was. He pulled Melinda aside. "Please tell me this time, what is the fourth dimension? Is it going to put her in a medical berth again?" He had seen what it took to pull through that shit. It was a dangerous way to spend all one's magic.

"It's complicated," Melinda said.

Raiden groaned. "Then fucking simplify it and tell me." He was fed up with all the secrecy. He needed to know everything about this world, but everyone was being a dick and avoided telling him anything.

"You know about the three-dimensional model, right? The fourth dimension is the fourth part of the actual principle, called the time and space dimension. With hyperdrive, we travel faster than light, but through the fourth dimension we can travel anywhere, instantly."

"That sounds too good to be true, and the last time Visaka did it, it left her at death's door," Raiden said.

"Yes. Unfortunately, the fourth dimension is filled with dark energy, which feeds the dark mages. It's like anti-matter for our magical energy. So, when we travel through it we lose our magic. As the caster of the spell, she had already used most of her energy to open the portal, so she was drained completely in transit." Melinda paused, frowning. "The mage emperor banned its use, but not many mages can use it to start with. Only a jumper mage can do it. I haven't seen anyone go through it other than the mage emperor and a few jumper mages who had the guts to do it."

Raiden turned this information over in his head. So Visaka was going to try to pull that jump off, and in the end, she would be exhausted like last time. That was one side of the equation, but how would the dark energy affect him? Last time, it hadn't affected him at all, maybe because of his own dark power. He hadn't known about it at that time, but now his powers had awakened.

"Are you sure this is a good idea?" His own demons haunted him. He was afraid of the effect this might have on his magic.

"I don't like it, but what other choice do we have? Visaka is wanted for a crime she didn't commit," Melinda said.

"Guys, we are jumping," Visaka said.

A dark shadow crawled through a tiny hole and started filling the space around them. The shadow extended its hands toward everyone except Raiden. Then he saw it. A large handlike figure slowly moved toward Visaka, and Raiden knew what that shadow wanted. It wanted the piece of magic that opened the portal. It was there to strip away Visaka's magic for days.

He wasn't sure what he thought about Visaka after learning she was a wanted criminal, but he knew she didn't deserve to be put on her death bed for attempting to save her crew. He had to save her from the dark shadow.

Raiden looked around. Everyone else was frozen in place. He jumped between the shadow and Visaka.

Then he heard her voice. Anna. His Anna.

"Baby, you're back! I've been waiting for you for so long. Come to me, Raiden."

His mind and heart were divided. Anna was calling him, but he had to save Visaka. As much as he wanted to go search for Anna in that darkness, he couldn't leave the others behind to die. Would his magic work on dark energy too? He took a deep breath and removed his armor. As soon as his left hand was bare, he could sense the darkness around him. He reached for it, sucking the darkness inside him. Glorious peace filled him, consoling his heart and soul. He craved this magic. He glanced down at his right hand, expecting to see the dark ring expanding, but instead it was shrinking.

What the fuck? Why is it shrinking?

Suddenly, the darkness around them vanished, and the light spread out. Raiden quickly put his armor back on, covering the black ring before anyone could notice it.

Their ship's consoles started blinking red and beeping as soon as they left the fourth dimension.

Melinda was the first to open her eyes. "Where are we?" she asked, looking at Raiden. "I guess your no-magic heart helped you get through the fourth dimension again. How long were we out this time?"

"Not long. We just came out of the fourth dimension. You'd better look at those warnings." Raiden pointed toward the alarms on the display.

Visaka stirred in the pilot's chair. "Whoa, where are we? What is happening here?" She pulled up a display to check on the alarms.

"We're screwed, Captain." Bradok said, still panting from magic loss. "We jumped into the middle of a damn space battle."

Chapter 35

VISAKA

Visaka rose from the pilot's chair. "How am I still breathing?" She felt different. Alive. Gone was the drained feeling she normally had for days after traveling through the fourth dimension. But how? This had never happened before. Not that she jumped through the fourth dimension regularly, but she'd made at least ten jumps in the last thirty years. That was a lot for any jumper.

"I don't know," Melinda said. "I feel fine too, maybe a little drained, but not much. Did we really jump through the fourth dimension?"

"Yes, but of course." Bradok said, his voice strained. "Did I mention the giant space battle out there? Eight dark ships, all cruiser class, are fighting with fifteen cruiser class Royal Navy ships under the direct command of the mage emperor." He tapped a button, and the ship's long range cameras came to life.

Visaka turned her attention to the display in front of her, which was focused on the two frontmost Royal Navy ships. She recognized one, the *Boomerang*. She had seen it once when its captain visited Titan. She had been on that ship, amazed by the blend of technology and magic on it. It had a magic receiver molded into every damn part of the ship. The ship's captain could literally fire a planet-destroying spell through that freaking ship.

Her ship was a small fish in a big sea. *Challenger* had a few magic receivers placed in the weapons system, and a few placed over the hull of the ship. Still, those receivers allowed her to control the ship for some time. *Boomerang* had a whole thirty-kilometer-long hull and hundreds of receivers placed over every corner of it. She'd wondered what Captain Melissa could do with that.

She had the answer in front of her. Captain Melissa was a fire mage, and she had made her ship into a freaking battle cannon. She shot a fire meteor, an advanced level six spell that was only taught to battle mages. Visaka knew about it, being a princess, but even she could never get her hands on such an advanced spell.

Her eyes darted to the dark ships. The one facing the *Boomerang* looked like a wide cylinder with two extra-large cannons placed at either side of it. It didn't act upon the meteor *Boomerang's* captain had cast. It merely sat there waiting for the meteor to hit it.

How naïve Visaka was to think that *Boomerang* would succeed. The meteor was intercepted few kilometers before it could strike the dark ship. Some dark mage had conjured a void shield in front of the ship, capable of discarding a level six amplified spell.

Visaka's whole body shivered at the thought of the magic that must have been used to cast the meteor and prevent it with a void shield. *Boomerang* had magnified it thousands of times for it to be strong enough to strike down another ship, but it was stopped by the dark ship easily.

Bradok shouted in amazement. "Holy grail, did you see that?"

Visaka understood his excitement. She felt it too. She had been a princess for years, but the only battles she had taken part in were after she became a pirate, and all those were small skirmishes. She had never seen a battle of this magnitude before. She was naïve and wrong thinking that magic was limited. Magic could be used any way a mage wanted with the addition of technology to it. The thought terrified her.

A couple small ships launched from one of the dark ships, heading toward them.

"Captain, what's our next move?" Bradok asked.

"What do they want from us?" Visaka wondered aloud. This was second time dark ships had followed them. What was so special about her that the dark mages were following her again and again?

Chapter 36

RAIDEN

Raiden watched every second of the battle in amazement. He had never seen anything like this in his whole life. Watching it made him realize how small he was. A ship as long as a ten-kilometer-long canal fired a meteor as big as a small asteroid. Fucking crazy, it was. And then the enemy ship put forth a void shield of impressive force.

The red dots on their screen started becoming larger as the small dark ships closed on them. The others were looking at Visaka expectantly.

"We travel back through the fourth dimension, on the correct path this time. I don't know what saved me from the dark energy last time, but I'm ready to do it again. Maybe God is helping us." She smiled.

What will happen if she gets to know about my dark powers?

He wasn't sure if he should tell her about it, but he was ready to help her again.

Visaka attached herself to the interface, and the darkness started pouring in around them. When everyone was frozen, Raiden moved toward Visaka, and when he stood next to her he saw his love. Two dreamy blue eyes smiled at him, calling to his heart. His love, his life, his Anna stood in the darkness, observing him.

"Anna..." He reached for her, but his hand only moved through dark energy.

"Raiden, at last! I can see you, my love. Come to me. Search for me and we'll be together again." Anna's voice soothed his aching heart.

Raiden remembered the evenings, the late nights he had spent listening to her for hours. He could do that again. Heck, he wanted that more than anything else.

"How, my love, how can I reach you? I can't even touch you." His voice cracked under the emotional strain. He had been constantly searching for a way to find her, but with every step toward her he stumbled over a new difficulty.

"I can sense you have the Crystal of Quantum."

He pulled the crystal out of his pocket and watched its glaring black light.

"The crystal is special and found near one of the God's weapons," Anna said. "It can be used twice to move through the dark dimension, but it has its limits. You can only move for a limited distance. Seek me out with the ship, and then I'll tell you how to use the crystal."

"Why can't I come right now?" Raiden asked, frustrated by her conditions. She was right in front of him. He could see her clearly, but still couldn't reach her.

"You're already on your way to somewhere else, and I'm busy too." Anna said. Her attention did seem divided.

"What's more important than us, babe?" She was giving more focus to something else, and he didn't like it. She clearly had power to come to this dark dimension, or whatever it was called. "Please Anna, come here now and we'll run away together, away from this mess." He was fed up with everything happening around him. He wanted peace and Anna, but he wasn't getting either.

"I'm losing the connection, Raiden. I can't keep this open forever." She waved her hand and vanished.

Raiden put the crystal back in his pocket. Showing it to anyone could get messy.

Why, Anna, why? Why did you leave me like this?

Chapter 37

RAIDEN

The ship jumped out of the fourth dimension in front of a huge red planet.

"Are we in the right place this time?" Raiden asked, still a bit out of it from the talk with Anna. He was happy and sad at the same time. Finally, he had found a way to get to Anna. His heart overflowed with joy as he remembered her face, her dreamy blue eyes, and her translucent skin. He missed her to the core of his heart. At the same time, he couldn't get to her right away.

Bradok cheered. "Yes! Finally."

"Why are you looking so happy?" Melinda asked, eyeing Raiden.

"Why shouldn't I? You guys are safe, and with your magic intact, too. And we didn't end up facing another clash of the titans. God, that battle was terrifying."

Melinda nodded, though her eyes were wary. "It worries me to see them fighting like that, especially with the display of dark magic power. Whoever cast that shield seemed to be too powerful to handle. I just pray that our navy gets out of it safely."

"Bradok mentioned the fleet was under the command of the mage emperor. Was it him firing that spell?" Raiden asked.

"No, this battle was nothing for him. He would be too busy to come and join a small skirmish like this." Melinda sighed.

Raiden nodded and studied the red planet visible on the display. "So, this is Alshat? It's huge." He was appraising its color when a large building with a narrow tower attracted his attention. It was tall enough to break through the clouds, visible even from space. "What's that?" He pointed at the structure.

"That's the planetary cannon. Fifty mages channel their magic through it, and it is capable of annihilating a complete fleet of destroyers," Melinda said.

"Why would they need that? This is a confederate plane, right? Aligned with the mage emperor?" Raiden couldn't believe a planet hosted such a large weapon. He surely hadn't see one on the Archaic world they had visited. Why would this planet require such a powerful weapon?

"No, it's not a confederate planet. This is one of the Legion worlds, previously named Spectra 34. They rebelled against the mage emperor a couple hundred years back, and since then the rebellion has spread to three other Spectra systems."

"Wow, I can't believe that politics has changed so much. It was way better on Earth. A few governments fought for supremacy, but none had such a powerful weapon. Of course, back then space threats were next to none."

"Power is a bad bitch, buddy," Cork said. "This world lacked the magic to create battle mages, but they made up for that in quantity. Other Spectra systems follow strict population control protocols, but these planets don't. In the end, a hundred low-power magic users can do the work of four high-level mages easily. And that's what they did." He paused. "It was worse when the rebellion took place, and I know it's still worse for these people. They are living on the verge of overpopulation, public resources are strained, people kill each other for luxury items, and still these bastards think they are supreme to our mage emperor," Cork said with anger.

"I know how that feels. Earth was in a similar position. I guess the extinction-level event taught humanity a lesson." In the States, he could get all the resources he'd ever dreamed of, but in countries like Afghanistan or other middle eastern countries, people didn't have basic things like clean water and homes. The Earth had truly been on the verge of exploding.

"Let's go and celebrate our victory, buddy. We ought to drink the strongest whiskey I have," Cork said.

"Whiskey? Real whiskey? Why the fuck you didn't tell me you had whiskey? I asked numerous times."

"Whiskey has to be earned, my friend, and I doubted you could handle it. But after seeing you foolishly try to absorb Ishita's ball lightning I knew you'd be fool enough to drink whiskey too."

"Speaking of Ishita, what was that marriage proposal about?" Raiden teased Cork.

Cork grimaced, but a faint hint of color stained his cheeks. Raiden burst out in laughter.

"Come on man. She was a lightning user. I'm a lightning user. It felt like a match made in heaven. You could say that her ball lightning pierced my heart." Cork chuckled. "Now let's go celebrate."

"Raiden, one moment," Visaka called to him before he could leave the control bridge.

"Yes, Captain?" He turned back to face her.

"What are your plans now?" she asked, looking him straight in the eye.

"My plans?" *I want to go back to Anna, that's the only plan I have now.*

"Yes, I promised I'd drop you on a neutral planet, and I guess this will do. I don't want you to be in any more trouble because of me." She sighed, looking around. "These guys have decided to go to the grave with me, but I don't want the same happening to you. You haven't seen our world yet, so go ahead and enjoy it while you are young."

She sounded like his nanny used to sound when he was a kid. Melinda had mentioned that she was thirty-one, three years older than him. Not that it mattered when you could live two hundred years.

Visaka continued. "So, I guess that's it then. We will leave for our meeting, and you can strike out on your own. I will give you some gold to get started, and you can find a job. There are still plenty of jobs out there for low magic users like you."

Visaka's words hurt. Raiden knew he would be leaving the ship soon enough, but he hadn't expected it to happen so soon. He had made good friends of Melinda and Cork, and he wanted it to last a bit longer. But hearing the captain's words, it was obvious that wasn't going to happen.

"Visaka..." Melinda began, but trailed off at a signal from Raiden. He suspected she may have intended to protest him leaving the ship, but he was fine with it.

"Thanks a lot, Captain, for saving my life numerous times. I'll get going in couple of hours. I hope that's fine with you." Raiden said.

This is what you get for saving these ones from the dark energy.

His evil mind started poking his good side.

Raiden decided he would try the black crystal as soon as he left the ship. He was angry enough to let these people go to hell.

Cork caught up with him while he was packing his stuff. Not that he had much, but he'd managed to buy a few things on Situla IV. A couple thousand years had passed, but humanity's choice in clothes had remained mostly the same. The only major difference he found was that mages preferred a long robe over whatever dress or shirt they wore.

"Hey buddy, why are you packing your stuff? I was waiting for you in my cube. Did you forget we were going to enjoy a round of whiskey?" Cork said.

"I'm sorry, Cork, but your captain asked me to leave the ship as soon as possible. So, I'll just fuck off from here," Raiden said, throwing the pants that wouldn't fit in his tiny bag on the floor. He'd never thought that he would have to move out like this.

"Are you kidding me, dickhead? The captain is not like that. She would never send you away from the ship. She was praising your battle abilities other day."

"I don't know what your captain thinks about me, but it was clear that she doesn't want me to stay on the ship."

"That's dumb. So, what are you going to do now?" Cork asked, showing an uncharacteristic hint of concern.

"I'm going to find a job, and then God knows what turn my life will take," Raiden lied, because he couldn't tell him he had access to the dark crystal and would be reuniting with his love soon. That would have set off all sorts of alarms in the minds of people who knew where Anna currently was. Someone traveling through the fourth dimension wouldn't be a welcomed thing for sure.

Cork stood there watching him for some time, but eventually shrugged. "I should bid you adieu then. All the best, friend, and hope to see you again soon."

RAIDEN WALKED OUT OF the starship after saying goodbye to everyone except Visaka. She didn't deserve it. He turned back to look at the ship one last time. He would miss it, for sure.

The first thing he saw when he walked away was a big checkout building. Apparently, everyone going to Black Core City had to register there first. At least he was given all the required instructions by Melinda before he left, so he passed the checkpost quickly and obtained a permit to work in the city. Back on Earth, he needed to get a permit to enter another country, but in this time the rules had changed. Now he needed a permit to enter a new planet itself. He felt tiny and insignificant. He had lot to learn and experience in this new world, and today was just the beginning.

He got directions from the planet's GPS system. One left turn and a mile of walking would take him to a train that connected the main city and its starport. When he was about to take the left turn, he spotted a hand coming out of a black hole.

Raiden quickly realized it was a portal to the fourth dimension. The hand came forward and threw a lightning wrap around him. His hands were tied behind his back. He tried to wrench himself free of that grip, but there was some invisible barrier around him.

Fuck, now what? Is some dark mage trying to capture me?

It shouldn't have been possible. Dark mages couldn't enter the human side of universe, but who else was capable of lurking in the fourth dimension?

Chapter 38

RAIDEN

While in the fourth dimension, Raiden tried to look at the person who'd pulled him in, but his neck was tied with the lightning barrier, so he couldn't. They got out of the fourth dimension quickly. The next thing he knew, he was falling. Thanks to his military training, he landed on his feet, unharmed.

He looked up and found two guys staring at him. "What's going on? Who are you? Where am I?" he asked, trying to grasp the situation around him.

"You're good, man." One of the men, the dark-skinned one, moved closer and studied him. "I didn't expect you to land on your legs so nicely."

"Yerra, I told you not to drop him like that. He is no good dead or unconscious before we can get the information out of him," the other man said. He was a petite white man, in his forties by the looks of him. But looks didn't deceive Raiden anymore. The man could be one hundred years old and just looked forty.

"What's the meaning of this?" Raiden asked. He sensed lightning energy coil around his neck and hands like a snake. Was that a side-effect of his dark magic powers, sensing the magical spells affecting him? "Why did you tie me up with magic?"

"Wow, you can sense the spells? Who would call you a novice mage? You have learned the ropes of our world quite fast," the white guy said, his face twisting a little.

"How do you know that?" Raiden took a step back. It bugged him that these guys already knew so much about him. How was it possible? He hadn't met more than fifteen people in this new world. Technically, he didn't even exist in the universe database.

"Does it matter to a dying man?" Yerra said, his face as expressionless as a rock. He waved his hand and a flashy yellow fireball appeared on top of his palm.

Raiden glared at the fireball. There was something different about it. The shape of the spell was like a water drop, narrow at one end and expanding into a ball-like shape at the other end.

"Why would you kill me?" Raiden tried to absorb a small amount of the barrier spell around him, and found it easy. He continued absorbing it little by little, weakening it to the point that he could get out of it with physical force. He wasn't bothered by any mages anymore. He had his own powers now.

"I don't like dark mages roaming free on our side of the universe," the white guy said.

A chill passed through Raiden. The man meant what he was saying. His eyes held a killing look.

"Who said I'm a dark mage?" Raiden said. "I don't even have aura lines in two digits. You can check that with the magic meter, if you want."

"Are you really trying to fool us? Do you think we can't detect the use of dark magic? This guy's gotta be a fool to think like this." Yerra almost rapped the sentence. "I told you, we should kill him and be done with this already."

"Who are you to decide whether I should live or die? You're dark mages too, right? You used the fourth dimension like you owned it. Now who's trying to fool who?" Raiden snapped back. He couldn't take this shit anymore. He absorbed the barrier completely but remained in the same position, waiting for the two to make the first move.

"He is feisty," Yerra said. "Aman, I think we should kill him already."

"Wait, we need the information first. Mister dark mage, how did you gain your powers without dying or transforming into one of the swarns?" Aman asked.

"Why do you care?" Even if he knew he wouldn't have told these guys. These guys had pissed him off already, and if he'd had the magic to cast a spell, he would have done it already just to shut these morons up.

"Aman, I told you, we don't need to know. Just kill him and get the artifact off of him." Yerra dashed toward him, and before Raiden could get his hands free, the man's right knee crashed into his chin, sending stars across his vision in broad daylight.

"What artifact?" Raiden spat blood on the ground. The guy was fast, he'd give him that. Even though Raiden was military-trained, he couldn't avoid that kick.

"We need the piece of the immortal dragon set you have," Aman said with a growl.

"What's so special about an armor piece? It's just a rusty old piece of metal." His armor was a bit special, but per Zumi it was just a piece of old equipment. Why would anyone want a magic suppressor? It made more sense for mages to focus on magic amplifiers, like the one he'd seen in the battle between dark mage ships and Royal Navy ships.

"You wouldn't understand. That's it, Aman. I'm going to kill him. One shot in the head and he'll be dead," Yerra said and fired the spell he was maintaining.

Raiden jumped. Even without the Mark V, he was quick, and the gravity on this planet was lighter than Earth, allowing him to jump higher and faster. The fire spell missed him by a large margin.

Aman pulled a pistol out of his pocket. It was quite similar to a revolver Raiden had used back on Earth, but it was hard to believe that a mage would use a mechanical pistol in this new world.

Aman fired a bolt of lightning from the pistol. It was quicker than Yerra's spell. Raiden couldn't avoid it, so he absorbed it with his left hand.

Yerra looked startled. "What the...? Aman, did you see that?"

Aman fired the pistol again. This time, the bolt stopped in midair and spread out into small threads of lightning, all targeting Raiden from different directions.

The spell closed on him in the blink of an eye, and he instinctively put both his hands out to stop it. Something happened inside him. His heart was filled with power he'd never experienced before. His right hand illuminated with lightning, and he fired a lightning bolt, the same as Aman had fired first. His lightning bolt destroyed the remaining threads of Aman's spell, which his other hand couldn't absorb.

What the heck was that?

"What did he just do? What is he?" Yerra freaked out, taken aback by the resistance Raiden was delivering. He fired a bigger fireball from his right hand, but Raiden absorbed it completely and fired it toward Aman.

Aman deflected it with his own equally powerful lightning bolt. He gasped and fired another lightning bolt at Raiden, which shared the same fate as the fireball from Yerra: the bolt was fired back at Aman.

"Yerra, fire on three!" Aman shouted as he deflected Raiden's spell.

Raiden was in trouble. He didn't have the power to absorb two spells at the same time, but he couldn't think of a way to avoid the situation. He had to try to absorb, even if it got his arm burned out.

Aman and Yerra each fired a spell. One was lightning threads, and other was the tear drop fire spell.

Raiden, think fast. Raiden's mind went into supercharged mode. On impulse, he tapped the button that connected the armor to his hand. The armor folded in on itself, turning into a small cube and falling to the ground.

The two spells closed on him, and struck his left hand one right after the other.

He wasn't sure what was going to happen, and he was half sure that his hand would get burned out. Another part of his mind suspected he would disintegrate completely.

Neither of these things happened. His hand absorbed both of the spells effortlessly, though his right hand started shaking with the power he had just absorbed. He knew that feeling, and pointed his arm toward Aman. His arm shot out a single spell, amplified by his own ability, a mixture of lightning swirling inside a fireball.

Aman was caught unexpectedly by the spell and fall like a stone, half burned and completely knocked out.

"Aman!" Yerra rushed to his friend's side .

Raiden grabbed his armor piece and his bag. He walked away while Yerra was preoccupied. He had to get away from them. But where?

Challenger.

Only his friends could save him if the duo decided to ambush him again.

He ran through several different possibilities to reach the ship as fast as possible before remembering the dark crystal.

She mentioned two charges. Why not use the first one?

He closed his eyes and thought about the ship, calling on the power of the crystal. When he opened his eyes, he was inside his cube on the ship.

Wow that was quick.

He rushed to Melinda's cube, but she wasn't there.

He rushed to control bridge, which was surprisingly empty. He walked to Cork's cube, but it was empty too.

Where is everyone? Did they decide to take a vacation or something?

He decided to leave the ship and look for his friends. He headed for the airlock, but when he touched the control panel he found a magical barrier around the ship, so he couldn't open the lock from inside.

What the heck happened here? Did they get arrested or something?

Chapter 39

VISAKA

"I will take Cork with me. The rest of you can take the day off," Visaka said.

"I should be the one accompanying you," Melinda said, resisting her proposal within a second.

"I'm not sure if that is a good idea. Richard was never fond of you back on Titan, and I don't want to agitate him, not today at least," Visaka sighed. Richard had never liked Melinda, while Visaka loved her for being a best friend rather than just a bodyguard. Richard always told her to keep her distance from Melinda, but she ignored him. It was his personal opinion, after all, and she didn't have to accept everything he said. Today, she was happy that she had never listened to him on this particular thing. He had discarded her as a criminal, while Melinda stood with her in every situation.

"Don't worry, Melinda. My axe is sufficient to take care of any trouble coming the captain's way." Cork glided his fingers over the blade of his axe. Visaka always wondered why he carried his axe everywhere when he was proficient in lightning magic.

"At least tell us what the rendezvous location is?" Melinda asked.

"I don't know," Visaka said. "I have a seed location where someone will be waiting for me. That someone will then take me to Richard."

"I don't like the sound of that," Melinda said with a concerned frown.

Visaka studied her, and all she found was care in her eyes. On Titan it was Melinda's duty to protect her, and even three years after they'd left the employer-employee relationship behind, Melinda still cared and guarded her. It all boiled down to true friendship in the end, and it always provided comfort to her heart that she had a loyal friend in Melinda.

"It's Richard we are talking about, Melinda. So, let's not doubt him. There was a time when I trusted him more than anyone in my life, and even today I feel I can trust him." *It's just that he wandered off the path we seek together.*

Melinda looked like she wanted to say something about it, but then she decided not to. She just waved at Bradok and they walked away, giving Visaka a relaxed moment. She'd expected more of a fight from Melinda, and not getting one eased her more.

"Just be careful, Visaka," Melinda muttered as she walked out.

"What now, Captain? When do we leave for the trap—I mean, meeting?" Cork asked, still sliding his thumb over the edge of his axe.

"Why do you even carry that thing?" Visaka asked, motioning at the axe. The question had long lingered in her mind.

"Meh, no particular reason." He smiled, showing his white teeth.

"Let's go, then."

VISAKA TOOK A LONG route to the rendezvous point. She wasn't sure why, but on the way she decided to heed Melinda's warning. She stopped a kilometer before the meeting point and scanned the location through her high vision glasses. She found no one but the regular crowd. It was a normal, busy day in Black Core City, and people were traveling to their jobs or elsewhere as usual.

"Everything looks good. We are clear to go," Visaka said while putting an air barrier around them both. She wasn't sure what to expect, but she thought putting something protective around them was prudent.

She wasn't wrong. A few bullets hit the barrier as soon as they reached the rendezvous point. A small drone hovered above them, firing metal bullets coated with water magic. Her barrier protected them nicely until Richard walked over. He waved his staff and destroyed the drone in the air. Legion worlds were infamous for their low-magic machines. The drone was one of them.

"What was that?" she asked as Richard closed in.

Her heart skipped a beat when she spotted Richard's strong chin and black eyes up close. She hated him for betraying her back on Titan, but seeing him so close started melting her resolve. He looked exactly the same as he had three years ago. Time had only added a little grump to his looks, and she liked it.

"Legion's specialty. It was a police autobot. Requires very low magic and can fire magically enhanced bullets from the air.

We'd better get out of here before another drone or a fleet of them attack us."

"But why did it come after me? I'm not a fugitive on this world," she asked.

"You're not, but I am. I recently joined the rebellion when my cover was blown. I'm helping them get their foot in the door here," he said as they walked away into a small lane. The houses on this lane were very much different from the large apartments they'd seen in larger lanes. These houses looked dirty and old, like a totally different class of people lived on these streets.

Richard leaned in to whisper, "Anyway, I will fly away from this dirty planet as soon as I get these morons settled in and start building the resistance against this fucking government." His lips brushed against her ear accidentally, and a sweet sensation passed through her whole body, reminding of her old times with him.

"Where are we going?" she asked.

"To a safe place. You can relax now. We are safe here." He smiled at her, as if the last three years didn't happen and might be just a dream. It bugged her.

Chapter 40

VISAKA

Visaka followed Richard, observing him quietly. He hadn't changed much. She could smell him from five feet away. He hadn't even changed his cologne, and it made her feel comfortable again, like she was in his arms.

She knew a spy's life wasn't easy. Nobody said it would be easy, but people still joined the secret spy academy and endangered their lives on distant planets. When Richard told her about his decision to join the spy academy, she was against it. She couldn't tolerate the thought of him dying on some distant planet. Richard joined the academy anyway and later settled on Alshat as a spy.

"How did your cover get blown? Bored of the job already?" she asked.

"Not exactly bored, but the stakes got high and I had to jump in to get this government overthrown." He smiled again. It set butterflies alight in her stomach, but why? Why did she feel like she was sixteen years old, just fallen in love again? She shook her head to clear it.

They walked through the dirty streets for ten more minutes and ended up outside a warehouse. The warehouse looked really old from the outside, but when they entered she found it more luxurious than expected.

Richard offered them a seat on a luxurious couch. She didn't even have a quarter of the luxury Richard had there.

"You have a nice setup as the rebellion's leader," Cork said.

Richard beamed at Cork, but it didn't feel like a natural smile. "So, tell me, what brings you here? You were cryptic when we spoke. Do you really have something to prove your innocence?"

Visaka was startled by his disinterested tone. He should have been happy, or at least cheered up for her. "First, tell me. Can you connect me with the King?"

"I can. But I hope you don't mind if I ask you to show me what you have before I initiate the communication. I can't ruin my credits and agitate him by putting a word in for you." He paused and looked in her eyes. "I hope you understand my situation here."

"That's fine." He was right. He would be putting his whole career in danger by asking the King to have a conversation with her. The King would definitely ask him why he didn't kill her on sight. Even though she was princess, she was a criminal in the eyes of the King.

"I have footage proving that my brother is alive and in collusion with the Legions. That proof should be enough to get me out of this mess." She could see the future. In a few days, she could go back to her home planet. She'd endured much hardship to prevent herself from being killed or captured by bounty hunters, and now she could rest peacefully.

Richard's stance changed. His features hardened. "Can I see that footage?"

She handed the data drive to Richard. He pulled up a portable display device and loaded the content. He watched the video carefully, his face turning darker with every moment of it. "Damn you Victor, they made a lot of mess back in the war of Ambala. Victor should have won that battle and bought a pride for Legion's armies. It was the first step in our plan."

"What are you saying?" Visaka's hand moved to her staff. If she was hearing what she thought she was, then she was in big trouble.

Victor walked out of nowhere. "He meant I should have won that bloody war."

"What the hell?" Visaka stood, pulling her staff up and calling upon her magic.

"That won't be necessary, Visaka. You are surrounded by five level five mages, and you don't want to mess with them," Richard warned her, pulling his own mini-staff out of his pocket.

"I'm not going down without a fight." Visaka fired a level five air bubble at Richard.

He deflected it easily with one swipe of his staff. "Do you really think that a mage can only reach level five? Do you even know there are more than level five mages? Trust me, my love, the academy is not the only place to learn those magic lessons." He chuckled.

Visaka took a step back. She never would've expected that Richard would know level six destructive magic. It wasn't taught in the academy. Only battle mages learned it on Spectra 1. But how did Richard get his hands on something like that? Nobody was supposed to know about it other than royal families and those who trained as battle mages.

Cork jumped in and stood next to her.

"Captain, this is getting dirty." He swung his axe, and a jet of lightning passed through his axe, spreading around and hitting both Richard and Victor.

"Now you too." Visaka's eyes widened. Cork had fired a level six lightning spread, a multi-level destructive spell. When did he learn it? And how did his axe act as a staff?

The spell stopped an inch away from Richard. He smiled at her, taunting her with his power. That bastard had been maintaining a shield around himself the whole time.

Victor wasn't maintaining one, so he took a direct hit and was thrown back against the wall. Cork's level six spell could have killed him easily, but Richard's shield had absorbed much of its impact.

The next moment, Visaka and Cork were overwhelmed by various spells hitting them from all directions. Richard wasn't bluffing about the five mages.

Visaka conjured magic to form an air barrier around them both, which deflected all the spells but at the same time left them without oxygen. She was prepared for that, but Cork wasn't. By the time she lowered the barrier, he was panting for air.

"I'm sorry for that, but it was necessary," Visaka said.

"I know." Cork put his hands on his knees. "Captain I'm getting you out of here. We can't win against this many mages. And for God's sake, don't come back." He touched her shoulder and the next moment she was standing in the middle of a road filled with many people.

Where am I?

It wasn't a street she had seen before.

Chapter 41

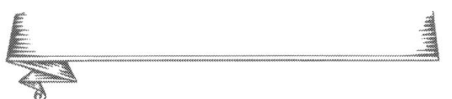

RAIDEN

Raiden wrestled with the panel, but it wouldn't budge. When he punched it in anger, he felt the magical barrier around the ship. He could feel the power pulsing through the whole ship, power capable of locking down electrical controls. He closed his eyes and focused on absorbing the spell, but it didn't work. Why not? He'd done it easily with the barrier spell Aman had put up, but something was different with this spell. Was it because of the metal between him and the spell?

Now what?

He dropped his armor piece in the hope that direct use of his power would give him an advantage, but it didn't work either.

"What the heck is happening with me?"

He tried again, harder this time, and felt magic energy pass through the metal. He instantly absorbed it. It was a massive amount of energy, and he released it with his right hand aimed at the door. The door was blasted with the amplified air spell, so powerful that Raiden was thrown back against the wall.

When the dust settled, Visaka, Bradok, and Melinda walked in through the hole he had just created.

"Raiden, what are you doing here? I thought you left hours ago," Melinda asked and helped him to his feet.

"I forgot something, so I came back, and when I tried to leave again, it was locked." Raiden said. No other reason to explain his appearance inside the ship came to mind.

Visaka eyed him suspiciously. "That doesn't make sense. But I don't have time to quibble. Melinda, get our smallest fighter shuttle out. We are going full offense."

"We can't do that. We are on Legion's military capital. They will shred us to pieces if we are caught," Melinda said.

"They already know about us. Why do you think our ship was locked?" Visaka bumped her fist on the wall next to her. "Don't worry, we will go in stealth mode."

"What's happening, Melinda? What are you talking about? And where's Cork?" Raiden asked, confused by their conversation.

"They have taken Cork, and we are not even sure if he is still alive." Malinda's eyes had an intense look.

"What?" Raiden couldn't believe it. "I don't know who we're up against, but count me in too."

"No way," Visaka said. "We may be going on a suicide mission, and I don't want you going down with us. This is my fault and I'm going to sort it out on my own."

"Cork was my friend too!" Raiden snapped. "Whether or not I fight for him isn't something you get to decide."

"He is right, Visaka. We should utilize his fighting skills in the Mark V. It would be an advantage for us," Melinda said.

Visaka looked at her, and then at Bradok. "Okay, go get rid of that ancient armor piece, and put on the Mark V. At least you would have some chance of surviving in that armor."

"Okay," Raiden said, without hesitation. It was time. He was ready to show his abilities to the others now. If they were going to save Cork, they needed every advantage they could get.

THE SMALL FIGHTER SHUTTLE had space for four people, and they all fit perfectly. There were multiple control panels for all four seats.

"Why are there so many control panels?" Raiden asked, wondering if it could be co-piloted from any seat.

"This ship is different," Melinda said. "Any person seated in it can pilot it or use the weapon system."

"Hmm." Raiden noticed Bradok sitting unusually quiet throughout the whole operation. Generally, he would have something to say.

He whispered to Melinda, "What happened to him?"

"Cork is his brother," Melinda whispered back.

Raiden's determination to save Cork grew.

"I have fed the location of their warehouse into the autopilot. We'll be going in stealth mode," Visaka said, and the threads of the magic-interfacer connected with her.

"I'm still amazed by the tech and magic integrations in this new world." Raiden stared at the threads. If someone had told him back on earth that magic existed, he would have laughed for starters, then made fun of that person. He'd believed that magic existed only in books. "I guess a couple thousand years can do wonders."

"Yes, it can," Melinda said. "And I bet we don't even know half of the things that exist. I feel magic is incomplete, as we still require machines to do interstellar travel, and only jumper mages can integrate with machines this complex."

"Is there anyone who can fly a craft without being a jumper mage?" Raiden asked.

"Yes, anyone with flight training can fly a starship and small fighters like this, but they can't use magic on a ship-wide level. Only jumper mages can utilize the full power of a ship's mechanics. The navy ship we saw, it had thousands of magic receivers installed on it."

"How many does our ship have?"

"*Challenger* has ten, and this one has four. Enough to kill tons of ships."

"Good. We're going to obliterate them with our magic." Raiden smiled for the first time since hearing about Cork. Visaka had told them there were seven battle mages there, and that had put them at great disadvantage, but with this ship they could win the battle. He might not even need to use his dark powers.

"Let's hope so," Melinda said. "Hush, now. Going in stealth mode means going quietly and slowly."

Everyone remained silent for the next half hour. They didn't want to trigger any alarms for the city police department, so they had to remain at subsonic speed. Soon, a grungy-looking warehouse came into view.

"We are reaching the warehouse," Visaka said. "I'm going to slice up the roof. Bradok, where are the heat signatures? I don't want to hit anyone."

"We are on top of the main hall. There is no one below it," Bradok said.

The ship hovered above the warehouse briefly, and then Raiden felt magic passing through the ship's outer edges to the spellcannon. The next moment, a big air bolt crashed into the roof and shredded it apart. Visaka used an air spell to pull the debris together before it fell, and threw it on an empty patch of ground nearby.

She's making sure it doesn't hurt anyone.

Raiden was proud of his captain.

"I'm detecting seven heat signatures, Captain," Bradok said. "Two are standing in the southwest room, but the others are moving toward the main hall."

"Captain, we are ready to jump in whenever you say." Melinda unbuckled her straps. Raiden followed suit, and so did Bradok.

"Wait for a moment." Visaka said.

They waited until two figures came into view. Visaka zoomed in on them and fired a spell that hit one of them square in the chest, piercing a hole through his body. The other one started, and then looked up at them. He had spotted the ship now. They'd had to come out of stealth mode to fire the spell.

"Go ahead," Visaka said.

Raiden, Melinda and Bradok jumped out of the ship. Bradok roared when he landed and shot a very large fireball at the enemy mage, who stood frozen in place beside his friend's dead body.

The enemy mage tried to jump away just before the fireball hit him, but he didn't quite get clear. Fire spread rapidly across his body, but a jet of water hit him and saved him from major damage. Two more enemy mages came into the picture, and two others joined them from the east side.

"Guys, the one on the right from the east side is Richard. He is the strongest one, so let me take care of him," Visaka said on comms.

Raiden nodded and jumped on the enemy mage that had been hit by Bradok's fireball. Melinda and Bradok engaged two others. Spells flew around the warehouse, water hitting fire, air hitting lightning, and soon everything went fuzzy.

Raiden decided to focus on his opponent, who was shooting fireballs at him. He wondered if fire was the most common magic power as he nimbly dodged incoming fireballs with the help of his battle armor. Raiden started moving forward, wanting to get close enough to the mage to get physical. If he could hit the mage without using his power, then he would prefer that. Ten feet away from the mage, he was clipped by a big fireball and caught fire. He quickly absorbed the energy inside him before anyone could notice it.

A few more steps, and I'll hit him with a straight uppercut.

Raiden's opponent's face twisted as he observed Raiden absorbing the fire. He shook his head in disbelief and started firing small fireballs rapidly before Raiden could get any closer. The speed of these fireballs was quite fast, and one of them almost hit Raiden before he could jump away. The mage stopped firing when Raiden jumped back. Perhaps the range on those smaller fireballs was limited?

Time to use my powers.

Raiden took a quick glance around to check on the others. Melinda had engaged a water user, and Bradok was holding steady against two fire users. Visaka was firing air spells through the ship at the Richard guy, and he was holding his own with his lightning magic. Before he turned to check on others, he spotted a large hole in the Visaka's ship, but she was holding the ship tight in spite of that. She was a skilled pilot. Everyone was nice and preoccupied with their own battles.

You chose the wrong opponent, my friend.

Raiden leaped forward. As soon as he came within five feet of his opponent, the mage started rapid-firing small fireballs again. Raiden quickly dropped to the ground, letting the balls pass over his head. Now he was just couple of feet away from his opponent. One more step. But his opponent was quick too; he channeled the next bunch of fireballs with his other hand.

He's good, but not better.

Raiden extended his left palm to absorb his opponent's fireballs. Three fireballs in, he stood eye to eye with his opponent.

"You must be wondering where the fireballs are vanishing," Raiden whispered.

The mage's eyes widened. "What in the hell—" Before he could finish, he was hit by an amplified version of his own spell. In a blink of an eye, he was reduced to ashes.

Raiden turned back to assist Bradok, who had already killed one enemy mage and was on the verge of killing another with a thick fireball to the face at a point-blank range. Melinda was succeeding too. Her opponent's clothes were sliced in many places, and blood oozed out of his body. But when Raiden turned to see how Visaka was holding up against Richard, she was on her knees, hands raised to maintain a shield to stop the lightning beam Richard was channeling. Raiden's eyes darted to their damaged ship crashed in a corner.

The shield Visaka maintained cracked under the pressure of the lightning beam, and Richard's lightning beam penetrated, aiming straight for Visaka's heart.

Chapter 42

VISAKA

The lightning beam, a level five spell, penetrated Visaka's level five air shield.

They say your past comes back to you moments before you die. Maybe that was what was happening to her.

"Richard!" She cried out in pain as her life flashed before her eyes. She was being killed by the one person she'd trusted more than herself once upon a time. They were together for years before splitting, and they'd shared everything—dormitory, books, food, bed—only to have it end like this. Then there was her father's face too, disappointed in her. As always.

I'm sorry father. I couldn't prove myself at the end.

She readied herself for death and waited for the beam to pierce her heart.

But the beam didn't hit her, and when she opened her eyes she found a man—Raiden—standing in front of her.

"Get out of here, you moron!" Visaka shouted. "Do you really think that puny battle armor of yours will hold against a level five spell?"

Raiden didn't move an inch. Did he intend to scarifice himself to save her?

No, that wasn't the case. When she looked closely, she saw Raiden was absorbing Richard's spell with his left hand. What kind of sorcery was that? How could he do that?

Then something happened that she never thought was possible. Raiden's right hand shook for a moment, then shot a nearly-exact replica of Richard's spell back at him. But there was something different with that lightning beam, a hint of purple mixed in.

Is that dark magic?

Her eyes darted to Richard, who was awestruck by Raiden's counterattack but quick enough to conjure a shield and deflect Raiden's spell.

"How did you…" Visaka couldn't believe her eyes. She had never seen a dark mage do that, and she knew every class a dark mage could born with.

"Stay back, Captain. I'm going to give him taste of his own medicine." Raiden sounded confident, something she'd never heard in his voice before. He'd changed a lot, and she was awestruck by his sudden change in attitude and his transformation into someone powerful.

Richard fired a lightning bolt that Raiden absorbed and sent back at him. Richard was being cautious now, only firing level two spells.

"I don't know what kind of power this man has, but you can't beat me with just his powers." Richard laughed and continued shooting small level two bolts at Raiden. At the same time, he advanced slowly on Raiden.

In an instant, the limitations of Raiden's power struck Visaka. All Richard had to do was hit Raiden at close range with his other hand, denying him the opportunity to absorb the attack.

"Raiden, he's trying hit you point-blank! We must think of some other way to beat him. Your powers without any clever solution won't work against him," Visaka whispered so only Raiden could hear her.

"How much power do you have left, Captain? I've got another trick up my sleeve, but I need the highest spell you can cast at me." Raiden touched his left hand and the armor he was wearing dropped on the ground in the form of a cube.

"Give up already, Visaka," Richard taunted. "I told you I have powers greater than a level five mage. I haven't even used half of my power yet. I'm going to kill you all, then show your corpse to the king and regain his trust. Once the army we are preparing on Alshat is formed, we will attack the Spectra worlds one by one. They won't even know what killed them. It will be the Imperial wars all over again."

"No! You are not winning this time." Visaka prepared a level five air bubble. If she could somehow manage to trap Richard in it, the bubble would suck all the magic and oxygen out of him, taking him down easily. But she couldn't guess what other power Raiden was ready to unleash.

"Do you really think his magic can kill me? You are naïve, Visaka. I've got a level six spell ready, and once I get close I will wipe you both from the surface of Alshat. Oh, and I forgot to tell you, your friend with the axe is waiting for you." He fired a lightning bolt at a nearby wall, destroying it and revealing a body without a head lying on the ground.

Reality sunk in. It was Cork who lay there, headless. Her heart cried out in a silent cry. She had spent years with that guy, and he was always something more than... dead.

"Cork, no—" A shout slipped out of her mouth, a tear of flame falling down her cheek. Richard was going to pay for this.

Raiden bolted toward Cork and found his head lying around a corner. He picked it up slowly and put it back near Cork's torso.

Then Raiden roared like a wild animal.

Chapter 43

RAIDEN

"Cork!" Bradok reached Cork's body in no time, and he knelt down with a lone tear dropping from his eye on his brother's face. He closed his eyes and roared something in an unfamiliar language.

Raiden's heart pounded faster as he contemplated how he was going to kill Richard. That bastard had killed his friend, and Raiden would to do whatever it took to kill that dickhead.

Bradok jumped to his feet, his eyes glowing with fire.

"Bradok, no!" Melinda ran to them, but when she touched Bradok her hands caught fire. She patted her hand against her leg to smother the flames. "Bradok, please don't do that. I promise we will kill him without it."

Bradok ignored her completely and continued walking toward Richard.

Raiden glanced at Richard, who eyed Bradok and stepped back.

"What's happing to him?" Raiden asked, confused. There was fear in Richard's eyes, and Melinda was obviously concerned.

"He is going nuclear," Melinda said, eyes bright with moisture.

"What do you mean?" Raiden watched Bradok, whose body now emitted flames, burning his own skin.

"He is sacrificing himself and casting a spell that will destroy him and anyone he touches. That's the final death of a mage of his caliber." Her eyes overflowed with tears.

Raiden made a snap decision and bolted toward Bradok, tearing his left hand out of the Mark V. If he was going to try this, he thought it best to do it bare handed.

"Raiden!" Melinda called him, but he didn't stop.

I won't let you die like Cork, buddy.

Bradok was moving slowly. His skin had all but vanished. Muscle and sinew was visible between patches of remaining skin, and even that was burning.

Raiden took a deep breath. He didn't know what would happen once he touched Bradok, but uncertainty wouldn't stop him. He grabbed his friend's shoulder, expecting flames to burn his palm, but instead he experienced intense magic, so intense that his body started shaking violently.

Bradok turned back and tried pushing him away, but Raiden held on tightly. If he let go, Bradok would be dead in no time. Raiden wasn't going to let it happen. He continued absorbing the spell.

A few seconds passed, and Bradok's flames vanished. Raiden felt immense magic building inside him, trying to get out. It was different than what he had experienced before, more of an angelic type of sensation. Something was special about this magic, and he knew now he had the power to defeat Richard, but he couldn't do that before absorbing all Bradok's magic. He let the magic swirl inside him and settle.

Bradok's eyes returned to normal, but his skin remained burned. It looked worse than a third-degree burn. Raiden had learned in Afghanistan that burns like that killed people, and there was nothing anyone could do about it. Raiden could absorb spells, but he couldn't heal Bradok. He might not survive after all.

Hopelessness built up inside Raiden. He wanted to save Bradok, but the spell Bradok had cast had already taken its toll on his own body.

Raiden closed his eyes as he absorbed the last bit of Bradok's spell energy. It was time for Richard to get his due. He opened his eyes and dashed toward Richard, who looked on with surprise on his face.

Surprise or no, Richard reacted quickly and fired a huge lightning beam at Raiden.

Raiden was ready for it, but before he fired Bradok's magic he wanted to look Richard in the eye. He searched for a trace of guilt in Richard's eyes, but there was none. So he fired all the fire magic he'd just absorbed toward Richard without hesitation. A beam similar to what Bradok had fired some time back emerged out of his right hand and crushed the lightning beam Richard had fired, then blew through the shield Richard had conjured around him. Just before Richard turned to ashes, Raiden saw fear in his eyes. Fear of death.

So, after all that, he feared his own death.

Raiden sank to his knees as the magic left his body, leaving him empty. His breathing became labored, and the last thing he remembered was Melinda rushing toward him.

"WHERE ARE WE?" RAIDEN asked when he regained consciousness.

"We are hiding in a room," Melinda said.

Bradok lay on the ground nearby, and Melinda held a palm over his body. She glowed with a yellow aura.

Raiden looked around but didn't find Visaka. "What are you doing? Is he alive?"

"He will survive but he'll be out of commission for days."

"Thank God." A large weight lifted from his chest. "What's that glow around you?" He noticed it changed intensity as the time passed.

"I'm healing him."

Raiden blinked, astonished. "You can heal people? Why do you need a medical bay if you can heal?"

"I can, but my healing works on spell damage effectively. For things like physical hits, it's quite useless," she she said.

"Hmm. Okay. Where's Visaka? And why are we hiding?" He saw Richard turning to ash, so there was no need for hiding unless they'd gotten into some other danger. "How long was I out?"

"She's looking for a way out. That bastard Richard summoned a spellbot before he died, and it's hunting us down. That's why we're hiding in this room. As for your last question, you were knocked out for ten minutes."

"That's comforting. It didn't kill me."

Visaka came back.

"How are you feeling, Raiden?" she asked.

"Better."

"Thanks for saving Bradok."

"I'm sorry about Cork. I should've come with you." He couldn't shake the feeling that if he had accompanied Visaka, he could have saved Cork.

"Hmm." She looked exhausted, and the death of her crewmate must have been taking a toll on her emotionally. "What is that power you have? When did you discover it?"

"When I fought with Zumi," Raiden said, glancing at Melinda. She looked disturbed hearing Zumi's name and her energy stopped flowing in Bradok's body for a moment, but she continued healing Bradok.

"You must have realized that it's dark magic, something you shouldn't be showing to anyone." Visaka was surprisingly cool about it.

"I tried that, but what's good is it if I can't even save a friend with it?" he asked.

"I guess that's true. You literally saved our asses today. Richard was too powerful for me." Tears flowed down her cheeks.

Raiden looked on in confusion. "Are you hurt? Why are you crying?"

"Calm down, Visaka," Melinda said, her voice harsh. "All along, he wasn't worth your attention. He was a bloody traitor. Admit it, you loved the wrong person."

Raiden finally understood what had really happened and why Visaka was so upset. He knew what it was like to lose a loved one. Even if Richard was dead now, it must be piercing Visaka's heart. He stood up and pulled Visaka into a fierce hug. That was the only thing he could do.

She didn't protest. She just kept crying for few minutes before pulling away from Raiden's embrace.

"Thanks, but I'm okay now." She cleared her throat.

"What's our plan now? What's a spellbot? Can we defeat it?" Raiden asked.

"We can't, at least not in this condition." She pulled a cube out of her torn jacket. The tears in her jacket showed her skin in many places, silky white skin that reminded Raiden of a baby's. She tapped the cube, and a holographic image popped up showing a bunch of large robots moving through a lane. They were not anything like what Raiden had seen before. They looked like something right out of a science fiction movie. Each had a gun attached to its left arm, while its right arm was hollow, like a canon mouth.

"What are those?"

"Spellbots. On Legion they are also called mage hunters."

"Mage hunters? I thought everyone in this universe has magic," Raiden said.

"They do, but Legion worlds are mainly made up of people who have very low magic."

"Low like me?" Raiden asked.

"No, if we speak about normal magic on a number scale, you have one while they have one hundred, and mages have ten thousand. These people can only conjure basic spells for day to day use. They can light a fire with fire magic, but they can't create a fireball out of it," Visaka said.

"So why do they have mage-hunting robots?"

"They were created to kill mages from other worlds. Only level five mages have a chance against them. They are made to resist magic."

"But how can they resist magic? Magic is nothing but an element, isn't it?"

"Yes, and no. Magic is nothing but the energy we can conjure. And we conjure it in the form of elements. These robots use antimatter shields."

"Antimatter? Now what's that?"

"It's a different theory altogether. It's the matter that is created around the God Weapons, and that is pretty much resistant to magic."

"God Weapons? You're confusing me now."

"Later. We need to get out of here and in our condition we can't defeat a bunch of spellbots," Visaka said.

Raiden thought about it. "I may have a way out."

Chapter 44

VISAKA

"Another thing you've been hiding from us?" Melinda sounded angry.

Visaka could understand why. Melinda always got a little touchy when she was dealing with anything about Zumi, her nemesis. Zumi had killed Melinda's sister, and since then Melinda had been after Zumi relentlessly. She'd thought she'd succeeded in killing her ten years ago, but recently on Situla IV she'd faced Zumi again, and Zumi was too powerful for her to defeat.

But that isn't the only thing you are hurt about, is it Melinda? Visaka knew Melinda trusted Raiden, had developed a special bond with him. Still, he'd kept them in the dark.

Visaka had had a special bond with Richard too, but how had that turned out? Betrayal, heartbreak? No, worse than that. He'd crushed her very existence, her pride, her trust. She should have been angry with Richard, but all she felt was emptiness.

I shouldn't be sad about his death.

She fought with herself constantly. She wanted to cry, but she wanted to control herself as well. She was confused. Until the moment Raiden hugged her for the first time. Then she just gave in to her feelings.

No, I'm not going to cry again. Richard was a traitor, and traitors deserved to die. But she'd loved him for years. She'd vowed to spend the rest of her life with him, but everything went to hell when she was framed for killing her brother.

Better focus on the current situation, Visaka.

She glanced at the axe she had brought with her when they'd decided to hide in a nearby house. She had suffered two losses today, but she was going to mourn only one.

Focus, Visaka. Focus.

The current situation demanded Visaka take action and get all of them out of there. But what should she do with Raiden once they got out?

When Visaka first saw Raiden using fire magic, she thought he had conjured a disintegrate spell to kill Richard. But it wasn't just fire magic. She had sensed strange dark magic coating the fire beam Raiden had fired, and that worried her. She remembered seeing fear in Richard's eyes for the first time in her life. It wasn't a level five spell that Raiden had fired. It was much more than that.

Is he turning into a dark mage?

He could have just teleported himself away, but he stayed and helped them.

What should I do with him?

He seemed to possess some sort of dark energy, but he hadn't converted into a dark mage. Whenever a human was converted into a dark mage, his appearance changed. He turned into a creature. Raiden looked human, and he had proved that he was as human as they were. She wasn't grasping the complete sense of the whole situation, but she was comforted by the thought that Raiden had saved Bradok, and for that thing she was willing to accept him on her crew. Yes, for the first time she thought to rely on a man she didn't like at first.

Visaka had used the last of her energy on a cloaking spell and seeking out the anti-mage robots, the weapon the Legion worlds were known and feared for. There was a reason that mage kings didn't wage war on these worlds, and this was the reason. Even though the mage kings would win the war, they feared their losses would be much more than it was worth.

There were four spellbots seeking them out, and there was no way they could handle all of them in their current state. Even Raiden with his dark power, which was still unknown to her, would fail against them. Unless, as he seemed to suggest, he had a trump card up his sleeve.

"I've got this." He pulled a black crystal from his pocket.

"What is that?"

"A teleportation device." His face illuminated with the strange light that the crystal emitted.

"Let me see it." Visaka took it, but as soon as her fingers touched the crystal she started losing the remainder of her magic. She yanked her hand back in shock. "This is made up of dark energy, and we can't touch it. We can't use this. We will be out of magic in no time, and we might end up in a mage coma." That was a big no-no in their current state. If she used the fourth dimension, she might put herself in magical coma. "Wait. The fourth dimension doesn't affect you, does it?" She raised her brows at him.

"No, it doesn't. Last time we jumped, it didn't affect you either. I made sure the dark energy didn't reach you." Raiden smiled. The bastard was enjoying his advantage.

"Come on, you gotta be kidding me. It's your personal teleporter? How amazing." Visaka couldn't believe this. "How does it work? We can't touch it."

"You can touch me, and I'll hold the crystal. It has a limited range, but I'm sure we can get back to our ship. I did it once before, when Aman and Yerra attacked me," he said.

"Wait, you know those guys too?" Visaka asked, surprised.

"Not exactly, but they recently captured me and wanted to kill me for being a dark mage. Am I a dark mage now?" he asked in an innocent tone.

"That's strange. How did they know about you? Even we never had any idea about it," Visaka said, but she wasn't completely sure about what was bothering her about these guys. "Those guys attacked me too, back on Situla IV. I wonder who they are." She looked back at Raiden and made a decision. "Remember you asked me for help to save your fiancée? I'm going to help you once we get some more crew."

"About that... I'm about to blow up the last chance I've got." Raiden looked at the crystal with sad eyes.

"What do you mean by that?"

"This is the crystal of Quantum. It has seeking magic built into it, allowing me travel through the fourth dimension, and I was supposed to use it when I was near her. There are only two charges, and I've already used it once." Shadows of regret covered his face. "Anyway, if we live we'll get some more chances."

Visaka was astonished by his choice. He was ready to give up his chance to meet his love. How could he be a dark mage when he had a heart of gold?

"Don't worry, Raiden. You are part of my crew now, and I will make sure that we get to her one day."

Raiden nodded, but there was reluctance in his eyes. "Let's go then."

Visaka and Melinda—with Bradok's unconscious body in her hands—held Raiden by his shoulders. Raiden muttered their ship's name, *Challenger*, and in a blink they were in the fourth dimension. For the first time, she could see the dark energies lying there. Also, for the first time, she wasn't losing her magic energy.

"Get ready to jump, guys. We are going through the fourth dimension again to get back to Venus. We need to retreat and heal." She glanced at Bradok, who was still unconscious, but his skin was almost healed now thanks to Melinda's healing magic, her specialty.

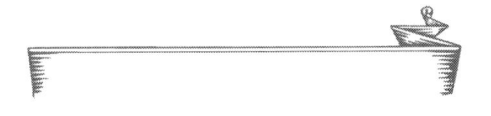

Chapter 45

RAIDEN

Raiden wasn't happy about using the last charge of his crystal, but he had no other choice. His friends' lives, not to mention his own, depended on it.

I'm sorry Anna, but I have to do this.

The moment they got back to the ship, Visaka said that they would jump back to Venus.

"I'm ready when you are." he said, "but can you jump right now? You're out of magic, aren't you?" Visaka looked exhausted, and he didn't want her to push herself.

"Yes, I can do one jump. I hope you won't let me die this time as well."

"I won't." He looked at his right hand and saw a second ring had appeared around his wrist. It was getting worse. "Let's go."

Level two dark mage?

"Melinda, can you check the outer door? I activated the nanobots before we left, and they should be done by now," Visaka said.

Melinda nodded and walked away. Ten minutes later, she came back and gave a green light. A few moments after that, they were looking at the First Vessel.

FOUR DAYS HAD PASSED since they had landed on Venus. Things were getting better for the first time. Visaka was getting back to normal, Bradok was healed, and their oxygen supply was refilled, too. Raiden had spent some time outside the ship, roaming the jungle and thinking about what would come next. For the time being, he was stuck with this ship. It wasn't that he didn't like being around these folks, but every day he spent on the ship was another day away from his love.

On the fifth day, he saw the captain back on the control bridge, doing something with the control panel.

"What's the plan now, Captain?" Raiden asked while he watched the nature and surroundings world on the Venus: it was beautiful and gave him a feel of Earth. The battle with Richard had been tiring, and he too had needed a break. He'd begun wearing the magic suppressor on his hand again, hoping to prevent any magic getting sucked into him. The second ring on his wrist worried him. He didn't want to be converted into a dark mage, not now and not ever.

"We jump to Titan and talk with my father. It's time that I come clean with him, and I have proof of my innocence now."

"I thought your drive was burned in the fight," Melinda said.

"I recorded Richard's conversation when we fought him. That should be sufficient testimony."

"Captain, we can't use the hyperdrive yet." Bradok said. It was the first thing he'd said in days. "The drive was hit when your spell blew off the airlock, and I will need more time to get it tweaked. This is an old ship, and it doesn't behave the way I would like."

"It's okay, Bradok. We can use the fourth dimension when we have our own dark mage." She looked at Raiden and smiled. "And don't you worry, Raiden, we will save her somehow."

"Let's jump out of here then," Raiden said. "It's not like I've got something better to do, like drink some whiskey." It would have been nice to find a drinking buddy and enjoy the evening without worrying about tomorrow or whatever darkness was coming for them. Anyway, he didn't have either whiskey or a drinking buddy, so why not get out of there?

Visaka connected herself with the magic-interfacer and initiated their jump through the fourth dimension, targeting Titan.

Raiden kept himself busy repelling dark energy away from his friends. He wondered how the two mages he'd met could use the fourth dimension. They were not dark mages. They'd used elemental spells, and they didn't have any dark magic energy associated with those spells.

A sudden jerk pulled them out of the fourth dimension.

"What was that?" he asked.

"I don't know," Visaka said. "Somehow, my magic was broken, and we got pulled out of the fourth dimension. Maybe the ship's word of power is broken. We can't forget this was the first model to feature these words, and it's a very old ship. Nobody uses these anymore."

"Where are we?" Raiden asked.

"We are one light year away from the battle scene, and I can sense the residue energy left by the battle," Melinda said.

"Ohh, back there again." Raiden's voice turned low. It was where he had last seen Anna, and talked with her.

"What's the matter, kid?" Melinda asked.

"I saw Anna the last time we jumped away from here."

"Was your fiancée on that black ship?" Visaka asked, curiously.

"Maybe. I don't know. But for the first time I could talk with her face to face. Before that, I could only hear her voice when we traveled through the fourth dimension."

"I've got a theory," Visaka said. "Anna must be using the fourth dimension to communicate with you, and she must have been in that ship to talk with you face to face. It makes sense. Earlier when we jumped, we were so far away from her that she could only call out to you. She must be trapped there, too."

"It does make sense, but we can't jump into a fleet of ten dark mage battle cruisers. We'd be shredded even before we reach there."

Visaka pointed toward the new control module that had been activated after their trip to Situla IV. "Come on, we have the new high-res module on this ship. Did you forget we can see one light year away with that thing?"

Raiden remembered seeing that after they got back from Situla IV and accidentally triggering the high-res cameras that magically showed them anything one light year away.

"Yes, let's check that out." Melinda walked to the display attached to the new control module and activated it. She focused it on the energy signature of the battle spells. "Guys, come here and check this out."

Raiden walked slowly over to her. He still regretted using the dark crystal, at least a little bit. But he didn't really have any other choice. Or did he?

One dark ship remained in a space littered with the debris of multiple ships. Raiden could identify some of the debris as belonging to the Royal Navy, as their design contained overuse of gold paint. Other pieces of debris were darker than black—those belonged to the dark mages.

"What do you think?" Visaka asked.

"I think the battle is over, and only one ship remains," Melinda said.

"What is the chance that Anna is on that ship?" Visaka asked.

"I don't know, but even if it's less than a percent I'm ready to take it." Raiden's heart filled with hope once again. There was possibility that he could meet his love again and save her from the dark mages.

Chapter 46

RAIDEN

"How do we proceed?" Raiden asked, his heart pumping faster than ever. If Anna was there, then he would have achieved his goal. "Can someone tell me already? I'm dying, here."

"We will use the second shuttle," Visaka said.

"I will get it ready." Melinda walked away.

Raiden looked at Bradok, who sat on a chair looking out at the void.

Visaka approached Bradok. "Bradok, can you maintain the ship?"

"Yes, Captain," Bradok said.

Raiden's heart went out to him. He had lost his brother and still he was there, ready to look after the ship.

Melinda prepared the shuttle, and soon they were flying toward the ship sitting in the debris field. They stopped just short of the debris field.

"Why do I feel like I've seen this before?" Raiden looked outside with the high-res camera they had. It was like déjà vu. They were next to a gas giant covered with red clouds and an asteroid belt circling it. It reminded him of the sixth planet of

Earth's solar system, Saturn. But Saturn was dead and frozen, so they had to be somewhere else. But where?

Raiden watched the dark ship burning in the debris. It seemed to be the fire of magic, otherwise how could a ship burn in space? It was very much a possibility that Anna was on that ship.

Time to find out.

"Visaka, we have incoming," Melinda said. Their shuttle's display popped up with a red warning.

"It should be easy to destroy it with magic, right?" Raiden asked. He had seen what the mages could do in a space battle. This should have been a piece of cake for Visaka.

"No, we can't. We are in a shuttle. It doesn't have enough receivers to amplify our magic. We are doomed. We can't even get back." Visaka sounded frustrated.

"Captain, can you try jumping through the fourth dimension? Is that a possibility?" Raiden asked.

"You can't jump in there." Someone else spoke.

Everybody turned to face that voice. Anna stepped out of a dark portal.

Raiden rushed to her. "Anna? I can't believe you're here. We were just coming for you."

She smiled and touched his face. Memories flooded him. This touch, this smell, he lived for this. She was his life, and this was what he'd longed for.

"Yes, Raiden. I'm here to take you back with me."

Raiden was snapped out of his thoughts. "Take me back? Where? Earth is dead, Anna." What was she really saying?

"Back to the master. Let's go, quickly. He is waiting for us, and he is not known for his patience," Anna said.

He looked into her dreamy blue eyes, but instead of innocence he found something else lurking there. Somehow, she was changed.

"Anna, who is this master, and why do you want to go back to him? You should be with me, my love. Why did you take so long to come back?" Raiden again searched her eyes to find the familiar innocent Anna, but he couldn't find her there. "Anna, what happened to you? Why is there so much darkness in your eyes?"

"Raiden, you have thirty seconds and two choices. Come with me, or die by the missile. It has been enhanced with void magic. Your friends' puny magic won't save them."

Visaka stood next to him. "Raiden, no! Don't go with her. She is not a human anymore. I sense pure dark energy coming out of her."

Raiden's heart pounded faster. He looked back at the others and knew what he was going to do. "Go back, Anna. Save your life. I'll be happy to know that you survived." He smiled at her, trying to give her assurance that he still loved her.

"If you aren't coming by your own free will, I will take you by force." Anna moved straight to Raiden.

"How could you think you can just take my crew member by force?" Visaka's voice rose in pitch. She stepped between them with a white air ball swirling in her hand.

"Do you really think that thing will intimidate me?" Anna giggled, and with a wave of her hand Visaka was thrown against the wall to her right.

"Anna, go back. I won't come with you," Raiden said, calmly. If the missile was going to kill everyone, then he would die with his crew. At least he had the comfort of knowing his captain considered him a crew member.

"Twenty-five seconds to impact," their shuttle's computer warned them loudly.

"Magita, stay there." A voice as dreadful as a demon's would be echoed through the ship. "I sense a very strong force coming to this position in ten seconds." A large man appeared from another dark portal.

Raiden's heart sunk in fear as the person stepped onto their ship. This person was something else. He had intense dark magic pulsing out of his body that forced everyone except Raiden to the ground. Raiden had to fight the urge to kneel and bow to him, but he succeeded.

"But master, he will die if we don't take him with us," Anna said.

"Enough, slave. I don't have time for your lowly emotions." He touched her shoulder and pulled her back into the dark portal.

Raiden helped Visaka to her feet.

"Who was that?" Bradok asked over comms. "His magic was so strong I could feel it from here."

Another dark portal opened. Visaka readied an air bolt in one hand.

A tall man with a subtle beard walked out of the portal. He too had an intense magical presence, but his magic had a soothing effect.

"My lord, Emperor Eric, thanks for coming." Melinda kneeled, and Visaka followed her.

"Raiden, get down." Visaka yanked his hand, and he fell flat on his face.

"What the fu—" Visaka's palm clamped over his mouth.

Her eyes shot fire at him. "You jerk, he is the Mage Emperor."

"Stand up, all of you. I've something to do." The Emperor said. He walked to the interface and touched it with both hands. A pulse of power passed through his hands, more energy than anything Raiden had felt before. This man had magic energy equal to the dark mage master, maybe more. The power level of these guys was so different. This man felt like a God of magical powers.

Raiden glanced at the nearby display unit and saw what the Emperor had done. He had shot a lightning bolt larger than their shuttle through the ship's weapon system. The bolt first wrapped around the incoming missile, then headed straight to the dark ship, destroying it in a blink. The ship shredded to pieces the moment the bolt hit it.

"Anna!" Raiden cried out. His love was dead.

"Don't worry, she didn't go back to that ship. Vakoxir took her somewhere else," the Mage Emperor said calmly.

"But Emperor Eric, how did you…?" Visaka asked.

"Get up, my love, and give me a tight hug first." The Emperor pulled Melinda into his embrace like a lover would pull another into his bear hug.

"What the fuck is going on here?" It was the first time Raiden had ever heard Visaka swear.

"Oh, you haven't told them yet?" The Emperor smiled at them, letting Melinda slip away from his hug. "Melinda works in the Emperor's spy force. But more than that, she is the love of my life."

"What?" Visaka looked at Melinda like she was going to kill her. "You were in the Royal Guard for ten years, and no one knew about this?"

"Can we talk about it some other time? You know it's not what it looks like." Melinda looked nervous and not happy with Emperor Eric's hand on her shoulder.

"God, I can't believe this," Visaka said. "This means the Emperor knows all of this, and about my brother too."

"Yes, I do. We have an extensive list of things to discuss. But right now, I've got to get back to my palace. People wouldn't like their Emperor slipping out of his bedroom in the night."

"What about us then?" Visaka asked.

"We will meet again soon." He smiled and vanished.

Raiden watched that God of magic disappear through the fourth dimension. It was a relief to know that his love was alive, but he was back to square one. He didn't know anymore if he would ever get her back. But at least he knew she had some humanity left in her, otherwise she wouldn't have asked him to come with her rather than simply taking him by force.

The End(To be continues...)

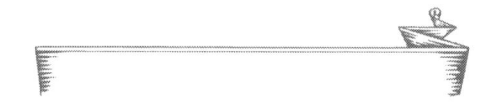

Magic System and Fun Plot Elements

MAGIC SYSTEM Developed in this book (As per the book 1) ... Blank space indicate that more spells will be available in next book/series.

Element	Level 1	Level 2	Level 3	Level 4	Level 5
Fire	Simple Fire	Fireball	Fire Blast		Disintegrate
		Fire Bolt			
Earth					
Water	Simple Water	Water Missile	Water Jet		
Light/Lightning	Simple Light		Orb of storm	Ball Lightning	Electric beam
Air/Wind	Simple Air push	Air Bolt	Air Scythe	Thick Air Ball	Air/Vaccume Bubble
Shadow					
Darkness					
Space					

Immortal Dragon Armor Power Levels... again this will be revealed further in next books/series.

Self Piece bonus	Requirement		Minor Power associated	Item bonus applied	
Left hand	Level one		Magic Suppression		
Right hand	Level two		Magic annihilation	Magic storage, Spell reducer	Next item bonus

224

STAR MAGE 2

Original Outline Planned...Not all things get written as planned, many things changed, many names changed (Like Raiden supposed to get a cybernetic arm, but instead he got a power-suit and set of armor). But I'm including this for fun...

1	Raiden wakes up on a station, where he sees couple of dark figured humans with animal features are inserting a rod inside Anna's neck. He try to get up, but can't. He watch in horror as Anna is hit by a lightning and when the light is about to explode, it goes back inside her and her eyes change. At the same time, few men and woman comes in and start firing spells out of their hands. And he fades up in the darkness.
2	When they visit the station, they find the dark mages run through with a woman, but find a man in the receptor pod lying around. She check him through magic meter, and he has no clear magic flow in his body, only two lines, and that two in opposite direction. Her first officer want to leave that person on the station, but Visaka decide to take him with them. Visaka takes the failed mage in human-tory reasons, even when her crew is saying not to help him because they are already low on resources. She wonders from where these guys have came. She has to decide on what her course will be next? And how is she going to survive with the low resources, and no where to go.
3	She wonders if she give Raiden a spell suit he might be able to use magic, or awaken him, losing her magic in the process. The spell armor fires a spell, that almost kills Melinda, saved by Vikasa. But even that fails, ans she looses all hopes she had to get a new battle mage onboard. She discuss with her crew, and ask Melinda to help him to adjust.
4	They move from there and land on Venus, the second planet in the Tabula one, Where the caption of the ship ask him to show his magic. He doesn't know how to fire it. She demonstrate and when he tries, nothing come out of his hand other than a spark. One crew member tells her a revelation of the man having only two magic lines flowing through his body in entirely opposite direction.
5	They are stranded on the Venus to replenish some of their supplies, and when no one is around, She tries to teach him magic, but that goes in vain. She show him her magic, but he is not able to replicate it at all.
6	They find a pirate sheep rotating around the Tabula one perimeter, and she decide to take on that. She easily cloak it under her spell, but now they have to enter and take control of the ship to get the resources.
7	They face another pirate ship, and watch how the caption menu-overs and use her magic to protect them easily. He wonder his role in all this, and how can he get out of this all. And where is his fiancé at that moment. They climb on that pirate ship, while one of the crew member gives him a battle armor and with that armor he is able to defend himself and save another crew member. he remembers his training on earth as a mercenary, and ask if they still usage rifles or pistols. The girl helping him tell him that it's there only in his pocket.
8	A clew, an old friend contacts her and say that he can help her gain her respect and powers back. But she has to meet him in the neutral zone so he can discuss this. She decide to fly through the fourth dimension to reach their fast
9	He discover about mages, and his questions are answered by the girl helping him. Caption ask him what he want, he says he want to save his fiancé. Caption says she has nothing to do with the Dark mages, but she can drop him on some neutral planet from where he can take his way. He is not sure what he can do anymore and what he will do on the neutral planet?
10	She gives a hope to Raiden that he can save his fiancé after hacking in the black mage network from the station.
11	Anna wakes up and find a power surging through her body. She wonder where is she, and meet Puller, the king of shifters who says that he came specially to test her power.
12	He sees a glimpse of a battle ship approaching their way, but he doesn't believe what he is seeing. He goes on practicing the defense spell with Melinda, which he some how manage to cast. But it's very feeble, and can't even stand a single blow from Melinda's hammer.
13	She face a small battleship patrolling and her first pilot usage a cloaking spell, exhausting himself and almost dying to save all.
14	When she is exhausted and recovering from her almost deathly situation, Raiden comes and tell her stories about his time in military and how was it to be on earth without mages and magic.
15	They land on a planet to buy some new tech which may save her ship for longer. She trade in her final sigil of the emperor of Tabula 33, her neckless which her mother had given her.

16	Melinda and Raiden goes to buy some help. They buy a neckless which can improve the magic flow a bit. It does help somewhat to Raiden and the get's some confidence. But when he tries to hit a electric spell, the spell backfires and almost hit Melinda. He is in depression of what can be done to get his fiancé back.
17	She faces a Dark mage fighter ship, which almost blow her oxygen recycling module before she could teleport with her ship further. Now her situation is more dire than anything else.
18	Raider's hand is severed when couple of dark mages teleport in their ship. Fighting with them in his battle armor, his left hand is heavily severed. He can't use it, but Richard (another crew member) fixes it with the spell armor suit hand. The cybernetic arm fix his muscle internally and he can use it now.
19	Raiden feels a strange sensation when he tries to pull a spell Melinda had recently taught him. He could get some sort of force shield reach out from his hands easily. He wonders and ask Melinda what is happening. Melinda suggest that maybe the spell armor hand is helping him cast the spell. But when they ask the same question to Richard he tells him that his magic lines in hand are broken, and hence the spell armor can functional normal as of now, and using the charged magic he had put in his hand to work. But he shouldn't be using much, as it may hamper his healing process.
20	He suggest using the Fourth dimension to reach her destination, and they accidently come out of the Fourth dimension to see the battle of shifters and royal navy before they jump back in the fourth dimension.
21	Anna is awaken and usage her power to demolish a royal navy ship. She is a Elite shifter now, skipping the Swarm phase completely.
22	They arrive at the neutral planet, where Raiden will go on his way with some money, Visaka offer him. She goes to planet with Raiden and Melinda, where her friend betrays her, and Melinda dies protecting Raiden. Visaka use her Instant transportation magic and send those both back to ship.
23	Melinda dies in his hands, and he sees the greatness of the Visaka. But now he has a way out, a message from his fiancé, Anna calling him to meet her at the edge of the star system, and give him a way to do that by a mystic courier which he can use one time to teleport anywhere in his side of the universe.
24	She is getting prepared for her Trial, which will put her to her death sentence. Her mother connects with her through an inter Tabula communication device, and ask why did she come back, and why didn't she go to the dark side and leave her life peacefully? She has no answer.
25	He seeks help from Melinda's brother, and start a small coup on the prison where Visaka is placed and saves her using his own magic for the first time. He get's a divination attack (his body lift in the air) and sees his fiancé working out a plan to snatch him from the Visaka.
26	Raiden has to go on Styder and save Caption, but he doesn't know how to do that, and he doesn't even have the magic to pilot the ship after the death of Melinda. He decide to use the mystic armor Anna send her and teleport to the prison where Visaka is imprisoned, and he usage the neckless and power armor together and teleport the whole ship with himself.
27	The final fight, where the situation is dire and Raiden usage his own magic to save everyone.
28	They discuss the future, and Visaka tell him that he has the dark mage power inside him. And the day's wouldn't be the same anymore.
29	They face another threat from the Dark mages, and now they are waiting for her.
30	Anna promises her master that she will have Raiden under her control soon. Master puller tell her that the Dragon emperor doesn't like failures, and he is seeking revenge on the children of Shiva.

Author Notes
Patricia Jones

To tell you the truth, I was done with writing. My last series didn't do well, and life happened, so I took a break and thought about permanently walking away from writing. But even though I tried, stories kept coming to me, begging to be written. One day a reader from India, a friend whom I met in my readers community, came up with a great idea. I couldn't say no to him, so here we are in the space fantasy genre. I had never read this genre before, but I love to read general fantasy and sci-fi. Also, I have A.P. Gore, an avid reader of Gamelit/Litrpg fantasy books, helping me out.

AP Gore

Ok, I am nervous. This is my first attempt at writing a book. Well, I didn't completely write it, but I played along with Patricia to complete this book. Thanks for reading this till the end. I don't have much more to say other than we are writing book two already, and there may be a third or fourth as well. Please review the book if you liked it.

Printed in Poland
by Amazon Fulfillment
Poland Sp. z o.o., Wrocław